FORT WAYNE
IS SEVENTH
ON HITLER'S LIST

FORT WAYNE

IS SEVENTH

ON HITLER'S LIST ❥

INDIANA STORIES

Enlarged Edition

BY MICHAEL MARTONE

❥ ❥ ❥ ❥
❥ ❥ ❥
❥ ❥
❥

INDIANA UNIVERSITY PRESS
Bloomington and Indianapolis

The paper used in this publication meets the minimum requirements of American
National Standard for Information Sciences—Permanence of Paper for Printed Library
Materials, ANSI Z39.48-1984.

MANUFACTURED IN THE UNITED STATES OF AMERICA

Library of Congress Cataloging-in-Publication Data

Martone, Michael.
    Fort Wayne is seventh on Hitler's list : Indiana stories / by
Michael Martone.—Enl. ed.
        p.   cm.
    ISBN 0-253-33687-2. —ISBN 0-253-20851-3 (pbk.)
    1. Indiana—Fiction.   I. Title.
PS3563.A7414F67   1993
813'.54—dc20   93-8645
1 2 3 4 5   97 96 95 94 93

For Theresa and now for Sam

CONTENTS

◆►

Preface

The first version of this book was called *Alive and Dead in Indiana*. It was published by Alfred Knopf in 1984. I had originally wanted to call that book *Biograph*, but the editors at Knopf nixed that title in favor of the one we used. That book contained the following stories: "Everybody Watching and the Time Passing Like That," "Pieces," "Alfred Kinsey, Alone, after an Interview, Dreams of Indiana," "Whistler's Father," "Dear John," "The Greek Letter in the Bed," and "Biograph."

When Indiana University Press issued the paperback edition in 1990, the decision was made to add several more of my stories, and the title was changed to *Fort Wayne Is Seventh on Hitler's List*. The stories new in that edition were "Fort Wayne Is Seventh on Hitler's List," "Three Postcards from Indiana," "Schliemann in Indianapolis," and "The Teakwood Deck of the U.S.S. *Indiana*."

In this new, Enlarged Edition, at the Press's urging, I have added four more stories, all, like their predecessors, dealing with Indiana. These stories are "Fidel," "On Hoosier Hysteria," "On the Planet of the Apes," and "On the State of the Union."

All of these stories are monologues; most are either narrated by or are about characters based on actual people, living or dead, who have had some connection with Indiana. I have wanted these stories to explore the relationship between fact and fiction as well as the intersection between fame and obscurity. I feel fortunate to have grown up in Indiana. The state is rich with its own stories and histories, another vital crossroads. I am fortunate too in that recounting the lives of these people and reconstructing the details of the places they inhabit seems relatively unexplored by many others in print. I hope these stories form a kind of Midwestern mythology adding to the complex web of anecdotes and tales we already tell ourselves about ourselves and about this part of the world that is our home.

Syracuse, 1993

Acknowledgments

The author wishes to thank the editors of the following magazines where the stories in this collection originally appeared.

Minnesota Review, Seems, Antioch Review, Shenandoah, Madison Review, Iowa Review, Antaeus, Gargoyle, Indiana Review, Story, Florida Review, and Windless Orchard Press. The Indiana Historical Society granted permission to quote from "Schliemann in Indianapolis" a journal created by Eli Lilly.

The author also wishes to thank the National Endowment for the Arts, The MacDowell Colony, and Iowa State University for support during the writing of these stories.

FORT WAYNE
IS SEVENTH
ON HITLER'S LIST

◆◆

Fort Wayne
Is Seventh
on Hitler's List

This is a city of poets. Every Wednesday, when the sirens go off, a poet will tell you that, after thirty years, Fort Wayne is still seventh on Hitler's bombing list. And you half expect to hear the planes, a pitch lower than the sirens, their names as recognizable as those of automobiles. Heinkels lumber out of the east, coast up Taylor Street, or follow the Pennsy from one GE plant to another. Stukas dive on the wire-and-die works, starting their run at the International Harvester bell tower, left standing on purpose, and finish by strafing the Tokheim yards. Junkers wheel, and Messerschmitts circle. All the time there would be sirens.

Grandfather keeps his scrapbooks upstairs in the window seat of the empty bedroom. When he dies, they are to be mine, and I am to give them to the Air Force Museum at Wright-Patterson Air Force Base. Grandfather started keeping these scrapbooks when he felt the time was right for war. He felt the war coming. In the years before the war, the scrapbooks that he kept were pieces of the world he found—a field outside of Peking where old people go to die, a man being buried alive, all the All-American football teams of those years, the bar of soap Dillinger used at the Crown Point jail, a man cut into three parts by a train, a Somalian warrior with no clothes on. These things made sense to Grandfather.

A real poet knows how to bomb his own city.

In the window seat where Grandfather keeps his finished scrapbooks, there is also his collection of missals, all the handouts from Wendell Willkie's campaign, and everything Father Coughlin ever wrote. The scrapbooks have interesting covers. There is one with a mallard duck on the wing worked into the leather. One is made of wood and has an oak leaf carved into it. Most, though, have only company names or *Season's Greetings*.

I have never been able to read all the scrapbooks. They are in no order, and nothing in them is. Every page is dated with the newspaper itself. He went straight through the book. One day I can read about the Battle of Britain, the next day VE day, the next the Soviet Pact. I have never gotten to the bottom of the window seat.

Once I found Hitler's list.

There are cottonwoods along the rivers. In the spring, a poet will look up at the undefended sky and announce, "At any moment we could be destroyed."

When I was little, I would practice making bomb noises, the whistling sound of a bomb falling. I would take a deep breath, form my lips, begin. I could make it sound as if the bomb were falling away from me, or on me, by modulating the volume, adjusting its fade or rise. I preferred the perspective of the plane, starting with the loud high note. A second or two of silence as the bomb is out of earshot. Then the tiny puff of air reaching me from the ground.

This is why old men smoke at night in the middle of parks. They do it to attract bombers.

Mother remembers certain things about the war. She remembers making dolls out of hollyhocks, taping butcher paper on the windows, and not being able to look at the newspaper until Grandfather had cut out the things he wanted. Once, in the A&P, she lost her underwear while waiting in line to buy milk. There was no rubber to hold up the underwear. She tells me this story every time I think I have troubles. Mother danced in the USO shows for the troops from Baer Field and Casad. Once she shared the stage with Bob Hope.

The whole city watches as the skywriter finishes the word.

S U R R E N D E R

Before going through the scrapbooks, I would sit on the window seat as if to hold the lid on. I would look out over the front lawn, across Poinsette to Hamilton Park. Through the pine trees and the blooming cherries, I could see the playground and the circling tether ball, the pavilion, the war memorial, the courts. I wasn't old enough to change the world.

At a high-school bake sale, the frosted gingerbread men remind a teacher of her students drilling on the football field during the war. They wore letter jackets with shiny white sleeves, or bright sweaters with stripes and decorations. They carried brooms at trail arms in the sunset.

How does evil get into the world?

Witches. Or children crying, "Catch me, if you can."

I watch Mother feed a baby. "Nnnnaaawwwhh," she goes, "here it comes in for a landing." She conducts the spoon on a yawing course, approaching. "Open the hangar door," she orders.

Mother looks at me as the baby sucks the spoon. "Remember?" she says.

"I remember," I say.

She sends out the second wave of creamed cereal.

In the fall, the new Chevrolets arrive, and Hafner sets up his old searchlight. It is surplus from the war, painted silver now. The diesel motor rotates the light. The light itself comes from a flame magnified and reflected into a beam. People come across the street to look. They look at the new cars lined up.

From Hafner's lot, you can look across the St. Joe River, south, to where three other beams sweep back and forth in the night. Those are coming from Allen County Motors, Jim Kelley Buick, and DeHaven Chevrolet. From the west is the lone light of Means Cadillac tracing a tight circle and toppling over into a broad arc, catching for an instant the tip of the bank building downtown and righting itself like a top. To the north is another battery of lights playing off one another, intersecting, some moving faster than others. Toward you and away. Bench's AMC, Northway Plymouth, Ayres' Pontiac. The illusion of depth in the night. The general vicinity of each source.

What are they looking for?

Something new is in the world.

*   *   *   *

There was a Looney Tunes cartoon Engineer John showed almost every day on his TV show. It was made during the war. Hitler, upset with the way the war is going, flies a mission himself, only to have the plane dismantled over Russia by "Gremlins from the Kremlin."

I would look through the scrapbooks to see how it really happened.

There has been a plane circling all day. There appears to be a streak of smoke coming from its tail. But I'm sure it's some kind of banner too high to read.

In the scrapbook with the wood cover, there is a picture of Gypsy Rose Lee selling war bonds.

This is the only picture in all of Grandfather's scrapbooks where he's made a note. It says: *I bet the Lord is pleased.*

During the war, the top hemisphere of the streetlight globes were painted with a black opaque glaze. They stayed that way after the war. No one seems to mind. Parts of dead insects show in the lower half of the globe. There's more and more of them in there summer after summer.

Grandfather read meters for his living. During the war, he was made block warden because everyone remembered the way he'd kept calm during *The War of the Worlds*. They also figured that he knew a little bit about electricity.

The city practiced blackouts all the time because they'd heard that Fort Wayne was seventh on the list. One night everyone stumbled into Hamilton Park for a demonstration. A man from the Civil Defense wanted to emphasize the importance of absolute dark, lights really out. Grandfather said that the man lit a match when the rest of the city was all dark. He said that you could see the whole park and the faces of everyone in the park. They were all looking at the match. He said you could see the houses. He said you could read the street sign. *Poinsette.*

The man blew out the match with one breath. The people went home in the dark.

Were they wishing they could do something about the stars?

They kept German prisoners in camps near the Nickel Plate yards. People would go out to the camps and look at the prisoners. Everyone felt very safe, even the women. Many of the prisoners had worked on streets downtown, or in the neighborhoods, and were friendly with the people.

Some of these prisoners stayed in town after the war. Some sent for their families. You ask them, they'll tell you—Fort Wayne is a good place to live.

In one of Grandfather's scrapbooks, there is a series of pictures taken from the nose of a B-17. The first picture is of the bombs falling away from the plane. In the background are the city streets already burning. In the second picture, the nose of another bomber is working its way into the frame and under the bombs, smaller now by seconds. The third picture shows the plane in the path of the falling bombs. One has already taken away the stabilizer without exploding. The perspective is really terrifying. The fourth picture shows the plane skidding into its tailspin. All this time the bombs are falling. And the fifth picture is the plane falling with the bombs.

Grandfather has arranged these pictures to be read down the page. One after the other.

*   *   *   *

Casad is a GSO depot built during the war just outside of town. I go there sometimes to watch them dust the fields nearby, the fertile strip near the bend in the Maumee. High school kids race by on the township roads on their way to Ohio to drink. I don't know if they even use Casad for anything now.

Casad was built to be confusing from the air. All you can see, even from across the road, are mounds of different-colored stones. Some of the piles are real, others are only camouflaged roofs. If you look closely at some of them, you can see a small ventilation pipe or maybe some type of window. The important things are underground. There are stories that date from the war of one-ton chunks of rubber in storage. They feared the damage that would be caused if they dropped any during transportation. Tin, copper, nickel, tungsten, and mercury were all supposed to have been stored there. From the road, quarry piles and sandpiper tents hump out of sight through the cornfield to the river.

It must all look pretty harmless from the sky.

The high school kids will stop on the way back. Late at night, they will sit on the hoods of their cars guessing which of the shadows are real. They are waiting to sober up and weave home.

Mother remembers his Prospero at the Civic Theatre. He lived here years ago. The only time I saw Robert Lansing act was on the TV show where he played the wing commander and flew B-17s. All I remember now are the shots in the cramped cockpit with the flights of bombers in the background. Most of the action took place on that tiny set, two seats and the man in the turret, aft, always moving as the actors talked or rocked from the flak or were riddled by "bandits" or feathered the number three engine.

Robert Lansing visited our high school and talked about acting.

He said there was a method that allowed him to use his past experiences in new situations. He said he was afraid to fly. He told us this standing in the middle of the gym floor, targeted in the cross hairs of the time-line.

In the stores downtown, there are bowls of lemon drops and cherry drops next to the cash registers. The merchants have broken into some of the supplies of the bomb shelters in the basements of their stores. They found that the water had soured years ago in the tins. The candy is sweet even though it is over twenty years old. They say the candy and water have been replaced in the bomb shelters. "No sense letting anything go to waste," they say. Every time you buy something, the person running the register will say, "Have some candy." And then they will mention where the candy comes from.

The small drums the candy came in are being used as wastebaskets. They are painted drab. Sometimes, the stenciled CANDY has been crossed out. The Civil Defense emblem can still be seen—the pyramid in the circle, pointing up to the sky.

Grandfather saw Bob Hope in the coffee shop of the Hotel Anthony. He showed him the clipping he had been carrying around for years, the one about Mother dancing in Bob Hope's show. Grandfather said that he wished Bob Hope could be home for Christmas but was grateful that someone did what Bob Hope did.

In the fall, the wind turns the trees to silent puffs of smoke.

Grandfather wants to know why I want to be a poet. He shows me a clipping of Eldon Lapp, who goes to our church. There is a picture of Eldon in his flight jacket and soft hat. During the war, Eldon was shot down over Germany. Before his capture, he lived for months in the Black Forest. He survived that long with the aid of another flyer who had been trained as a Boy Scout and had been in Germany during a world jamboree. This flyer knew all the tricks—how to fish with a line and makeshift hook, how to conceal a trail, how to secure a camp, how to read signs. Eldon swore then that if he got out of this alive he would dedicate his life to scouting.

"That's vocation," Grandfather says to me.

The Kiwanis Club sponsors airplane rides all summer. Taking off from Baer Field, the tour flies over most of the city. I saw the Wayne Knitting Mill's tall smokestack, *Wayne* built right into the bricks. I flew by the elevators, followed Main Street downtown and circled the courthouse. Then over the Old Fort, looking defenseless, and the filtration plant with the ponds. I followed the Maumee from the three rivers downstream, sweeping by the old Studebaker plant, Zollner Piston, all the wire-and-die works, Magnavox. Then banking up the bypass, north, over the shopping centers and malls and their parking lots, over Eckrich and the campus, to my house.

I could see my house. I knew it even from the air. There were people in the front yard I did not know, looking up, shielding their eyes, waving.

Grandfather, all you can see are the contrails. The plodding lines of the bombers and the lyric corkscrews of their escort. It is how this city chooses to die. Daylight raids, everyone is watching. This is the American Way. To see it coming. The bombs are inverted exclamations at the beginning of their sentence.

                          *   *   *   *

I can hear the planes looking for the city each night. I keep my eyes closed as they fly over the house. Their engines pulse like the sirens. It is a patient sound. And I wait too.

I wait for them to drop the flares, or for a few of them to come in lower. We did not ask for this. They fly by overhead. You can hear them, but you cannot see them. They are showing no lights. Low clouds. No stars.

They go on, on some heading to the west. But they will be back later. Then, further east, there will come the panting sound, almost comic, as they drop the bombs randomly, hoping to hit something, and then, empty, go back to where they came from.

Tarsk and Hartup have been taking aerial photographs for years. All the merchants and the schools, each new mayor, every public place has one of their pictures. Sometimes the picture is of one building and at other times of whole blocks. There are calendars, too, that everyone gets from Lincoln Life. In Mike's Car Wash people will try to find their house in the picture that hangs in the lobby while their car is being dried. Every day Tarsk and Hartup fly over the city taking pictures—but no matter what picture you look at, someone will always point out what is missing, or what has since disappeared.

◆✦

Three Postcards
from Indiana

SANTA CLAUS

"A watch means that conditions are right for a tornado." As we
drove, I explained the difference between a watch and a warning.
This was her first summer in Indiana, and every time she turned
on the radio she found herself in another depression, pressure
dropping. An imaginary line extending just north of and passing
through the counties of La la la and Mmmmm. The Balkan states
of the weather map. It would be in effect for a couple of hours.

"Is that us?" she said.

"It's just a watch," I said, and I told her what to look for, though
I had never seen one myself. I remembered sightings, hearing
of funnels over towns. One Easter. One Palm Sunday. "If you
see one, we get in a ditch. Some place low." I remembered
feeling this way every spring and summer—too hot, too still.
You can hear better. There was this picture in the grocery store
encyclopedia of a drinking straw driven into the trunk of an elm.
She had seen violent storms in Baltimore but only the leavings
of hurricanes, not this kind of wind—all eye and finger, one
that can see and feel.

Of course, it started raining, and the voice on the radio tracked the storms, interrupted by the sizzle of static—soft or loud, close or far away. I'm here now, the static said. Teasing. Moving.

"It's not us," I said.

In the half-light we passed the statue of Santa Claus, melted limestone, in a field surrounded by broken skeletons of farm implements slick with rain and submerged in mud. Horses, startled by the lightning, shied and ran sideways away from the sound. The book said the statue said: For the Children of the World.

Triple A just mentioned the St. Nicholas Inn, the only motel in Santa Claus. It was made up of little bungalows, Munchkin-size, scattered behind a gas station.

"A mite windy," said the woman, letting us into number 3. The baby riding on her hip yelped each time it thundered. "No one stays here. They drive up from Louisville or down from Naplis to see Santa Claus. My baby sees him every day."

We went into our room and found everything half-sized—the TV, the end table, the bed. "Think," she said, "to grow up seeing Santa Claus every day but Christmas." Yes, in the part of the world where flying is easy—lawn deer, flamingos, silked jockies.

As we slept did we shrink? Were we that small? Did our feet touch the ground? Did we count each other's sheep as they clouded that tiny room? We heard the baby cry all night through the storm.

The next morning I knew the sky was clear before she pulled the drapes and turned on the morning news. Eyes still closed, I heard that a tornado had touched down in the Baltimore zoo the day before. A woman reported that she survived by being blown into the hippo house. A miracle. The world is full of miracles. Closing my eyes again, I see the woman blown into the hippo house. One puff, a blow to the belly, arms and legs trailing, millions of shrimp swimming backwards into the hippo house. Size has no scale. I am asleep again.

Later we wrote our postcards in the car, parked next to the

post office. The doors were open. To keep the post office, the natives changed the name of their town from Sante Fe to Santa Claus. Now, besides the amusement park, the post office is the town's only industry. All the letters come here. All the ones addressed to the North Pole. All the lists. All the directions home. We came here to mail some from the eye of the storm. All the stamps were airmail. It is too hot for Christmas, too still. You could hear the sleigh bells.

"Look. Look." I said, pointing across the evaporating parking lot to the back gate of Santa Claus Land, "Santa Claus." In shirt sleeves and bermudas, he swung a black lunchbox as he went to work. He was sweating and he wasn't whistling. She didn't look up.

"Where?" she said.

But he was already gone through the gate and hidden behind the scraps of newspaper caught in the cyclone fence. I pointed with my finger.

"There."

FRENCH LICK

We came into the valley from Santa Claus and skirted the grand hotel fronting the road, a walled city. We crossed the old Monon tracks, the spur where the private cars from Chicago were switched right up to the door of the resort. "Monon," you say. I told you again about Hoosier, who's there. The French in Indiana. We stayed down the road in a motel—half in French Lick, half in West Baden. Alsace-Lorraine. "A lick," I said, "was for the wild game. The seasoning in the ground." I will show you the salt blocks in the supermarket.

"Kiss me, there," you said.

We walked back over to the grand hotel. In the coffee shop you had a tongue sandwich, and the waitress behind the counter said I was the first to order a bagel and cream cheese "since I've worked here. What do I do?" Next to us on the little stools, a couple argued about the food. She complained about her peas in French. He scolded her in English. We came for the waters you said. But really you only wanted your postcards canceled with French Lick. We played Space Invaders in the arcade, and they kept coming. Then, we lingered on the veranda, following the deck chairs to the spring. The spring was in a gazebo, bubbling through a pool of green water. "Kiss me, here," you said, but the sulfur smell was too strong. "If nature can't Pluto will." You read the sign. "This is what they came for?" you said. "This is what they came for, the presidents and gangsters?"

The next morning you wrote your postcards, naked, at the desk. Maids were making up the next room. I watched David Letterman on TV as he made jokes about Muncie. Turning, you said, "Let's," licking 10 cents Justice, "go there next." On my way to the shower, I stopped behind you. You were writing that animals need their licks. The sounds you make, the ones that are not quite language, name nothing.

"Knock, knock," I say in your ear. "Who's there?" you say from another world.

MUNCIE

In Muncie, we are staying at the Hotel Roberts, downtown. And, though the elevator is automatic, they have a man wearing a Nickel Plate conductor's hat who pushes the buttons. We have learned that the third Middletown study is in progress. We are mistaken for sociologists by the old men we sit with in the lobby when we watch TV. Before we can quiet them with the truth, they are speaking of their church affiliations and bathroom practices.

The first night here, we ordered a pizza by phone from a campus take-out to be delivered to our room. Since then we have gone through the yellow pages for anything that will be delivered. When it arrives, Theresa answers the door wrapped in the hotel bath towel. After awhile we begin to receive all sorts of things we never ordered—pints of macaroni salad, goldfish cartons of fried rice, heads of lettuce. They are delivered by college boys wearing Ball U T-shirts, who then sculpture obscene animals with the warm tin foil. Everything seems to have the same tomato paste base.

If we leave the Roberts at all, it is to watch the summer basketball leagues play on a court next to one leg of the high school drag. The cars go by honking. The players glisten in the single scoop lamp. The backboard is perforated metal used in temporary runways. The hoop is a red halo with not even a metal chain net dangling from the rim. Or we go to the Ball factory and watch them make mason jars, press the rubber lips to the tin lids. They have shelves of jars the Ball brothers canned seventy-five years ago. The seal holds stewed tomatoes with yellow seeds, embryonic eggplants, black butter chips and sweet gerkins no one will taste, okra, of all things. We have been there several times, and unlike other factory tours, there is nothing to sample unless we care to can and wait a season. We do keep our loose pennies in a Ball jar, and Theresa makes the boys reach in it for their tip, a monkey trap. They can't withdraw their clenched fist through the narrow mouth of the jar without letting go of the money. She leaves them laughing, closing the door against them with the flat of her foot.

But all of this is typical here, or, because we do it in Muncie, it is typical. We have seen the sociologists on the sidewalks, shielding their eyes with their clipboards, trying to cross the street. They take pictures of barber shops and trophy stores. Or they sit and count cars in and out of the parking lot or look for butts beneath their feet. In every room there are questions to be answered with special pencils. "What brings you here?" In each case, love. We write that our dream is to open all the jars one at a time and to eat vegetables older than our grandfathers. We want everything delivered to us. Theresa wears nothing but two pasties of pepperoni. I am reading books on pickling. The scientists will figure out what is going on here.

◆▸

Everybody Watching and the Time Passing Like That

Where was I when I heard about it? Let's see. He died on that Friday, but I didn't hear until Saturday at a speech meet in Lafayette. I was in the cafetorium, drinking coffee and going over the notes I had made on a humorous interp I'd just finished judging. The results were due in a few minutes, and the cafetorium was filling up with students between rounds. I had drama to judge next and was wondering how my own kids had done in their first rounds. So, I was sitting there, flipping back and forth through the papers on my clipboard, drinking coffee, when Kevin Wilkerson came through the swinging doors. I saw him first through the windows in the doors, the windows that have the crisscrossing chicken wire sandwiched between the panes. He had this look on his face. I thought, "Oh my, I bet something's happened in his round." He looked like he'd done awful. But he'd probably flubbed a few words or dropped a line or two, or so I thought. I once judged a boy making his first speech who went up, forgot everything, and just stood there. Pretty soon there was a puddle on the floor and all of this in silence. The timekeeper sat there flipping over the cards. So I spoke up and repeated the last thing I could remember from his speech. Something about harvesting the sea. And he picked up right there and finished every word, wet pants and all.

They were corduroy pants, I remember. He finished last in his round, but you've got to hand it to the boy. I'd like to say the same kid went on to do great things. But I can't because I never heard. So I tell this story to my own kids when they think they have done poorly, and I was getting ready to tell Kevin something like it as he came up to the table. Kevin was very good at extemp. He's a lawyer now, a good one, in Indianapolis. He said to me then, "Mrs. Nall, I'm afraid I've got some real bad news." And I must have said something like nothing could be as bad as the look on your face. Then he told me. "Jimmy Dean is dead. He died in a wreck."

They'd been listening to the car radio out in the parking lot between rounds. That's how they heard. "Are you all right, Mrs. Nall?" Kevin was saying. Now, I'm a drama teacher. I was Jimmy's first drama coach, as you know. I like to think I have a bit of poise, that I have things under control. I don't let myself in for surprises, you know. But when Kevin said that to me, I about lost it, my stage presence if you will, right there in the cafetorium. Then everyone seemed to know about it all at once, and all my students began showing up. They stood around watching to see what I'd do. Most of them had met Jimmy the spring before, you know, when he came home with the *Life* photographer. They just stood watching me there with the other students from the other schools kind of making room for us. Well, if I didn't feel just like that boy who'd wet his pants. Everybody watching and the time passing like that.

But you were wondering where I was, not how I felt.

I suppose, too, you'd like to know how I met James Dean, the plays we did in high school, the kids he hung around with and such. What magazine did you say you're from? I can tell you these things, though I don't quite understand why people like yourself come looking for me. I'm flattered—because I really didn't teach Jimmy to act. I have always said he was a natural that way. I think I see that something happened when he died. But something happens, I suppose, when anybody dies. Or is born for that matter.

I guess something is also gone when the last person who actually knew him dies. It's as if people come here to remember things that never happened to them. There are the movies, and the movies are good. It's just sometimes the people of Fairmount wonder what all the fuss is about. It isn't so much that the grave gets visited. You'd expect that. Why, every time you head up the pike to Marion, there is a strange car with out-of-state plates, bumping through the cemetery. It's just that then the visitors tend to spread out through town, knocking on doors.

Marcus and Ortense, his folks (well, not his parents, you know), say people still show up on the porch. They're there on the glider, sun up, when Ortense goes for the *Star*. Or someone will be taking pictures of the feedlot and ask to see Jimmy's bedroom. Why come to the home town? It's as if they were those students in the cafetorium just watching and waiting for things to happen after the news has been brought.

People are always going through Indiana. Maybe this is the place to stop. Maybe people miss the small town they never had.

I'm the schoolteacher, all right. I remember everyone. I have to stop myself from saying, "Are you Patty's little brother?" Or "The Wilton boy?"

That's small town.

The first I remember him, he was in junior high. I was judging a speech contest for the WCTU, and Jimmy was in it, a seventh grader. He recited a poem called "Bars." You see the double meaning there?

He started it up kneeling behind a chair, talking through the slats of the back, you know. Props. It wasn't allowed. No props. I stopped him and told him he would have to do it without the chair. But he said he couldn't do it that way. I asked him why not. He said he didn't know. He stood there on the stage. Didn't say one word. Well, just another boy gone deaf and dumb in front of me. One who knew the words.

I prompted him. He looked at the chair off to the side of the stage.

Couldn't speak without his little prison. So he walked off.

"Bars" was a monologue, you see. In high school, Jimmy did a monologue for me, for competition. "The Madman." We cut it from Dickens.

We took it to the Nationals in Colorado that year. Rode the train out there together for the National Forensic League tournament. As I said, it was a monologue. But it called for as many emotions as a regular interp which might have three or four characters. You never get more than five or six characters in a regular reading. But Jimmy had that many voices and moods in this single character. Could keep them straight. Could go back and forth with them. He was a natural actor. I didn't teach him that. Couldn't.

I know what you're thinking. You think that if you slice through a life anywhere you'll find the marbling that veins the whole cake. Not true. He was an actor. He was other people. Just because he could be mad doesn't mean he was.

You know the scene in the beanfield. Come to the window. There, you see that field? Beans.

They used mustard plants in the movie.

And here, we know that. Jimmy knew that too. Beans are bushier. Leave it to Hollywood to get it all wrong.

In the summer, kids here walk through the beans and hoe out the weeds. They wear white T-shirts and blue jeans in all that green. Jimmy walked too when he was here.

That's the town's favorite scene. Crops. Seeing that—those boys in the bushes, white shirts, blue pants. How could he have known how to be insane? Makes me want to seal off those fields forever. Keep out everything. You can understand that, can't you?

It was quiet then. Now the Air Guard jets fly over from Peru. I notice most people get used to it. At night, you can hear the trucks on I-69 right through your bed. I lost boys on that highway before it was even built. They'd go down to the Muncie exit and nudge around the barricades in their jalopies. Why, the road was still being built, you know. Machinery everywhere. Imagine that. How white that new cement must have been in the moonlight. Not a car on the road. This was before those yard lights the rural electric cooperative gives the farmers. Those boys would point their cars south to Indianapolis and turn out the lights, knowing it was supposed to be straight until Anderson. No signs. No stripes on the road. New road through the bean-fields, through the cornfields. Every once and a while a smudge pot, a road lantern. That stretch of road was one of the first parts finished, and it sat there, closed for years it seemed, as the rest of the highway was built up to it along with the weight stations and the rest stops.

I think of those boys as lost on that road. In Indiana then, if you got killed on a marked road, the highway patrol put up a cross as a reminder to other drivers.

Some places looked just like a graveyard. But out on the un-finished highway, when those boys piled into a big yellow grader or a bulldozer blade or just kept going though the road stopped at a bridge that had yet to be built, it could be days before they were even found.

The last time I saw Jimmy alive, we were both driving cars. We did a little dance on Main Street. I was backing out of a parking slot in my Buick Special when Jimmy flashed by in the Winslows' car. I saw him in the rearview mirror and craned my neck around. At the same time, I laid on the horn.

One long blast.

Riding with Jimmy was that *Life* photographer who was taking pictures of everything.

Jimmy had on his glasses, and his cap was back on his head.

He slammed on the brakes and threw his car in reverse, back-ing up the street, back past me. He must have recognized my car. So out I backed, out across the front of his car, broadsiding his grille, then to the far outside lane where I lined up parallel with him.

He was a handsome boy. He already had his window rolled down, saying something, and I was stretching across the front seat, trying to reach the crank to roll down mine on the passenger side. Flustered, I hadn't thought to put the car in park. So I had to keep my foot on the brake. My skirt rode up my leg, and I kept reaching and then backing off to get up on one elbow to take a look out the window to see if Jimmy was saying something.

The engine was running fast, and the photographer was taking pictures.

I kept reaching for the handle and feeling foolish that I couldn't reach it. I was embarrassed. I couldn't think of any way to do it. You know how it is—you're so busy doing two things foolishly, you can't see through to doing one thing at a time. There were other cars getting lined up behind us, and they were blowing their horns. Once in history, Fairmount had a traffic jam.

The fools. They couldn't see what was going on.

Jimmy started pointing up ahead and nodding, and he rolled up his window and took off. I scrunched back over to the driver's side as Jimmy roared by. He honked his horn, you know. *A shave and a haircut.* The cars that had been stacked up behind us began to pass me on the right, I answered back. *Two bits.*

I could see that photographer leaning back over the bench seat, taking my picture. I flooded the engine. I could smell the gasoline. I sat there on Main Street getting smaller.

When the magazine with the pictures of Jimmy and Fairmount came out, we all knew it would be worth saving, that sometime in the future it would be a thing to have. Some folks went all the way up to Fort Wayne for copies. But Jimmy was dead, so it was sold out up there too.

I wasn't in the magazine. No picture of me in my car on Main Street. But there was Jimmy walking on Washington with the Citizen's Bank onion dome over his shoulder. Jimmy playing a bongo to the livestock. Jimmy reading James Whitcomb Riley. Jimmy posing with his cap held on his curled arm. He wears those rubber boots with the claw buckles. His hand rests on the boar's back.

Do you remember that one beautiful picture of Jimmy and the farm? He's in front of the farm, the white barn and the stone fences in the background. The trees are just beginning to bud. Tuck, Jimmy's dog, is looking one way and Jimmy the other. There is the picture, too, of Jimmy sitting upright in the coffin.

Mr. Hunt of Hunt's Store down on Main Street kept a few coffins around.

That is where that picture was taken.

In Indianapolis, they make more coffins than anywhere else in the world. The trucks, loaded up, go through town every day. They've got CASKETS painted in red on the sides of the trailers.

You wait long enough downtown, one'll go through.

See what you have made me do? I keep remembering the wrong things. I swear, you must think that's all I think about.

What magazine did you say you were from?

Jim's death is no mystery to me. It was an accident. An accident. There is no way you can make me believe he wanted to die. I'm a judge. I judge interpretations. There was no reason. Look around you, look around. Those fields. Who could want to die? Sure, students in those days read EC comics. I had a whole drawer full of them. I would take them away for the term. Heads axed open. Limbs severed. Skin being stripped off. But I was convinced it was theater. Look, they were saying, we can make you sick.

It worked. They were right.

I'd look at those comic books after school. I'd sit at my desk and look at them. Outside the window, the hall monitors would be cleaning out the board erasers by banging them against the wall of the school. The air out there was full of chalk. I flipped through those magazines, nodding my head, knowing what it was all about. I am not a speech teacher for nothing. I taught acting. I know when someone wants attention. The thing is to make them feel things before anything else.

I taught Jimmy to kiss.

I taught Jimmy to die.

We were doing scenes from *Of Mice and Men*. I told him the dying part is pretty easy. The gun George uses is three inches from the back of Lenny's head. When it goes off, your body will go like this—the shoulders up around the ears, the eyes pressed closed. He was on his knees saying something like "I can see it, George." Then *bang*. Don't turn when you fall. After your body flinches, relax. Relax every muscle. Your body will fall forward all by itself.

Well, it didn't, not with Jimmy. He wanted to grab his chest like some kid playing war. Or throw up his hands. Or be blown forward from the force of the shot.

"Haven't you ever seen anything die?" I asked him.

"No," he said.

"It's like this," I said, and I got up there on the stage and fell over again and again. I had George shoot me until we ran out of blanks. It was October, I remember, and outside the hunters were walking the fields flushing pheasants. After we were done with the practice, we could hear the popping of shotguns—one two, one two. We hadn't noticed that with our own gun fire.

Hunting goes so fast and that's what irritates me.

Jimmy was so excited, you know, doing things you couldn't do in high school. Dying, kissing. That's how young they were. Kids just don't know that acting is doing things that go on every day.

"Just kiss," I told Jimmy after he'd almost bent a girl's neck off. "Look," I said, taking one of his hands and putting it on my hip, "close your eyes." I slid my hands up under his arms so that my hands pressed his shoulder blades. His other hand came around. He stood there, you know. I tucked my head to the side and kissed him.

"Like that," I said.

I quieted the giggles with a look. And then I kissed him again.

"Do it like that," I said.

Even pretending, Jimmy liked things real. No stories, action. He was doing a scene once, I forget just what. The set for the scene called for a wall with a bullet hole. Jimmy worked on the sets too. I was going to paint the hole on the wall, and Jimmy said no. We waited as he rushed home. He came back with a .22, and before I could stop him, he shot a hole in the plywood wall.

I tell you, the hole was more real than that wall. I remember he went up to the wall and felt it, felt the hole.

"Through and through," he said. "Clean through and through."

The bullet had gone through two curtains and lodged in the rear wall of the stage. I can show you that hole. If you want to look, I can show you.

Right before he died, Jimmy made a commercial for the Highway Safety Council. They show it here twice a year in the driver's education class. The day they show it, I sit in. The students in the class each have a simulator. You know, a steering wheel, a mirror, a windshield with wipers that work, dials luminous in the dark.

Jimmy did the commercial while he was doing his last picture. He is dressed up as a cowboy, twirling a lariat. Gig Young interviews him. They talk about racing and going fast. Then Gig Young asks Jimmy, the cowboy, for advice. Advice for all the young drivers who might be watching. And I look around the class, and they are watching.

It is the way he begins each sentence with "Oh."

Or it's the lariat, the knot he fiddles with.

That new way of acting.

What is he thinking about? Jimmy was supposed to say the campaign slogan—*The life you save may be your own.* But he doesn't. He looks toward the camera. He couldn't see the camera because he wouldn't wear his glasses. I can see what is hap-

pening. He is forgetting. He says, "The life you save may be"—
a pause—"mine." Mine.

I guess that I have seen that little bit of film more times than
anyone else in the world. I watch the film, and he talks to me,
talks to me directly. I have it all up here.

He kissed me.

He died.

Leave his life alone.

I know motivation. I *teach* motivation. I teach *acting*.

◆▸

Pieces

I parked that night in a lot across the street from a restaurant I wanted to call on the next day early. I had gotten into Fort Wayne late, having driven all day from my home in Corbin, Kentucky. I had made a side trip crossing the Ohio at Brandenberg to Maukport, then on to Henryville, Indiana, where I was born and grew up. It was for old times' sake. No one knows me there now. I talked with no one. Climbing north, I had this sense of things starting up again. It was already hot. They were running, and I took my place in the stream of white-haired travelers hauling those silver trailers, driving those new finned cars, passed only by Negro children being driven south out of the cities to Grandma's place on the land in Mississippi or Alabama. These are the times of real migrations. With the warm weather and those new highways, people had started to move. I was on the road all the time and hadn't seen anything like it. Not since the thirties.

The traffic put me late in the city. I got my bearings from the bank building downtown. I'd been here before a few years earlier in 1950. I found Anthony Street, and followed the overhead trolleybus lines, a main street, and must have even followed a trolleybus because I remember thinking they still have these, the smell and the sparks and the sound of sliding metal. Fake lightning. And there might have been real heat lightning that night and lightning bugs.

The elms looked real sick in the streetlights. I didn't have time to find a place, or money if I had found one, having not much more than enough for gas and a bit extra, just in case. Nor am I so inclined. I like sleeping in a car, especially my car. I have my spices. And there was a change in the weather that night. So when I spotted the Hobby House Restaurant—and I had some trouble since it was locked and dark—I pulled into the lot across the street which had a huge sign still on that late. It was a painter's palette with three brushes poking through the thumb hole. Each dab of paint was lit up by a different color of neon.

It wasn't a paint store but an ice-cream parlor. Each color a flavor of ice cream, I guess. The sign burned and buzzed to high heaven, but I was able to settle down in the backseat with beaten biscuits and my scales.

I weighed my spices and herbs in the pools of colored light for the next day's meeting.

The palette was on some type of timer.

At midnight, it went out and silent just like that, even though no one was around to switch it off. And there was lightning that night but no thunder. It flashed as I put my things away in the dark.

Am I telling you too much? These things might not be to the point of the matter. But give me a little room to build up speed.

I'm sixty-six years old, which should give me a pretty good enough excuse to act this way.

I can remember fifty years ago as if it were yesterday. I can't remember yesterday.

The maps in my time you had to read. *Three miles from the county line, turn left on the macadamized road, an old Indian trail, and at four and a half miles, with red barn on the right, take another left. This is county road 16. Oil mat.* Roads weren't lines then. Give me time and I'll make the turn.

I sell a recipe for fried chicken. That's what brought me to

Fort Wayne that night. I used to have my own place in Corbin, and I couldn't complain. Business was good because my cooking was good. Country ham, black-eyed peas, red-eye gravy, okra and string beans, watermelon pickle, hoe cake, baked apples. Duncan Hines wrote me up in his *Adventures in Good Eating* before the war. Gave directions. The shed on your left, the fence on your right. That kind of thing. He got you right to my door. No Worcester Diner, tablecloths, and gravy boats. And the thing was in place. I even had a root cellar with roots.

Eisenhower's defense highways put me out of business. I sold it all for a big loss. My wife said that it was about time we went south anyway, and she wanted to head down that new 75, a clear shot to Florida. SEE ROCK CITY on every barn and birdhouse. But I wasn't going to manage on my Social Security wearing Bermuda shorts, thinking twice about buying this pack of Beechnut gum.

A few years ago, I taught a good friend of mine, Pete Harman of Salt Lake City, how to fry chicken with this recipe and every indication was that the chicken did a job for his business.

There are some other places too. Other men who have heard about it. They would send me four cents, a nickel a bird. But it was nothing I worked at or thought about. And now these cars were passing my place. Though I couldn't see the traffic, I could feel its steady rumble through my feet. Those roads are so big you can hear things like you can over open water.

My last good days were feeding the crews who drove the graders and dozers. Their hard hats were lined up on the rack by the door like skulls. I'd rather wear out than rust through. So I got on that road, joined the rumble with the Pete Harman deal in mind. I put a pressure cooker, the spices and scales, my apron and knives in the backseat of my '53 Pontiac. It had an amber Indian head on the hood, and it handled like a boat. I shipped out over that sound.

It was no great adventure. I'm an old man, after all.

I started by cooking for my family. Time to get out of the kitchen and take it on the road since the road had up and gone.

It's not so strange. You fellows are fretting right now about what to do with your folks, I bet. I had to make up my own mind, had to make a little money.

So I hadn't met her yet. Instead, I am in a parking lot in Fort Wayne, waiting for this restaurant to open up for breakfast. A crew of high school kids is tarring and repainting the lot. They are making noise as they close off a section with rope laced through the handles of gray sealer cans. I'm the only car in the lot. It's a big lot. They lay down the parking stripes that look like fish bones on the tar. I can see the painter's palette sign is turquoise. Down the way is the baseball stadium where the Pistons play. There are big silver pistons on the press box. I know beyond the stadium is a road being built.

The elms look even sicker in the daylight. More like willows than elms. The restaurant has the look of being open now, though I haven't seen anyone unlock the doors, and, sure enough, cars start turning in. I start mine and drive across the street carefully as the traffic is picking up. I park and go in. I like the place. The walls have stained, knotty pine paneling. The tables have red checkered tablecloths and each, no matter how large, is set for two. There are wagon wheels on the walls; half-wheels are buried in the backs of booths; the chimney lamps on the tables rest on little wagon wheels. The coffee is streaming into pots.

In the restroom, I wash my face and shave quickly. I have very little beard. The room is well lit and clean. Before going back to my booth, I knock on the women's restroom door. When there is no answer, I peek in. It's the same story, clean and bright, a couch for nursing.

It is a breakfast menu. Combinations of eggs, ham, potatoes. They have steak, hash, all the juices, and a specialty—a doughnut with its hole teed up in the center, glaze dripping from one to the other. But I order lunch—a hamburger, fries, and a Coke.

"No problem, hon, but the deep fryer's not on till eleven. Hash browns okay?"

Everything is fine.

There's a regular clientele. Coffee is poured before anyone asks. Conversations are picked up where they left off the day before, morning papers left behind to be picked up. So are large tips. There are men in uniforms. They use their fingers and dip their toast. They stack their own dishes. This feels like home.

"Here, let me heat that up for you," the waitress says, pouring coffee with a smile.

Even though it is crowded, it is comfortable. There are dining rooms closed off. I can just sit, drink the coffee, and read your local news.

After the morning rush has left for work, what remains are the old men talking about the weather, a feeble-minded boy sweeping up, and my waitress with the bright glass coffeepot still steaming in her hand. I ask to see the owner. I know his name. At first she looks at me as if I've betrayed her hospitality. Then she reads me as a salesman, smiling as she says, "All right, I'll get him, wait right here."

The owner comes through the swinging doors, out from his office. He is followed by my waitress, who brings him coffee as he sits. I get right to the people we know, talk about the National Restaurant Association, mention the new highways. He's at a disadvantage when I make my pitch. I could be his father. I ask him to let me make some chicken for him. What's he out but some shortening and flour? That's right. I stayed on to cook for him and then for his customers. Then we shook on it, and I taught his people in the kitchen how to do it. Next thing was to make arrangements for getting the ingredients mailed and him sending all the money back home.

It wasn't until I was back on the road again that I saw her hitchhiking. At first, I thought she might be a boy. She wore pants and had her hair up short. She had a small roll at her feet, a silver frying pan tied up on it. She stood, thumb out, too far from the road. But I saw her. She grabbed her things and ran to the car and opened the door without looking in first.

"Where you going?" I asked her.

"Wherever you are."

Fair enough. I put it in gear and got back on the highway. It didn't take her long to notice.

She said, "Jesus, what's that smell?"

I told her what the smell was and what I was doing on the road. I didn't ask anything because I felt she didn't want me to, nor could I tell from her looks whether she had been on the road for a while or if I was her first ride. She didn't say a word when I pointed the car toward Michigan. Maybe she didn't know. Maybe she didn't care.

It seems to me there aren't any real crossroads anymore for most people. Most of us are going against the grain. She had nothing to decide, only tendencies. I had taken her up. Your part of the country is a funnel of flat land with a bias. I worked as a ferryboat captain on the Ohio. A small boat. Ferried autos and walkers from Jeffersonville to Louisville. I made the trip once an hour, seven hours a day. I heard about Mark Twain and read some of his books. I wanted to be a river pilot like him. I took to wearing white suits like his. Piloting that boat, you could feel what I mean. The Ohio wants to sweep you west.

She said, "You're from the South, aren't you?"

I said that all depends on what you mean. Some people will say the South starts at 38th Street in Indianapolis.

The accent, the funny suit. I knew she was thinking of it all. The greasy diet, the in-breeding. I don't mind. On these trips, I let people think what they think. It's good for business. My age helps too. But I try not to go on about what I've done or seen. Let them imagine what they want.

I'd say she was a city girl. Movie stars on her mind. She probably thought the road led somewhere, that it was not just for the nation's business, the national defense. The "big road," you call it in Kentucky. The road to town. The road that leads to something different. As I think of it now, I didn't understand her half the time. She was restless on the seat, read the road signs to me, wanted to play games with license plates. I said she should follow along on the maps I keep in the glove box. She didn't want to.

There were things I didn't want to be with her but couldn't help being because they are what I am. An old man, a salesman, a gentleman, her father. But she needed to be talked to. The country whizzing past needed to be filled up with fun. I have advice, though I try to hide what I mean. I've done my share on posses walking through field stubble and dragging rivers while dogs bawled. Maybe I wanted to scare her, but I say I didn't.

She put on her sunglasses so I couldn't see her eyes and slouched in the seat against the door. It wasn't locked, but I held off from doing anything about it. We went on miles that way, me lecturing. She leaning into the unsafe door. Finally, I reached across the seat behind her. Pushed the button down. She didn't say a word except "Thank you."

We were traveling through the lake country near the Michigan line. The trees along the road would open up to water. I talked about me then. I couldn't help myself. I had made a sale. Like that waitress, I just wanted everybody served. I left home when I was twelve. I told her that I had worked on farms, been a streetcar conductor, was in the Army in Cuba, worked jobs that disappear. I studied law by mail waiting on the ready track of freight yards. Boiler was my light. I was a justice of the peace in Little Rock. Sold insurance and tires. Headed the Chamber in Columbus, Indiana. You can check that out if you want. I'm not really from the South, you see. Not from anywhere.

"Yes," I said. I pulled it all together, a piece here, a piece there. Yes, I have seen things. I rode the reefers and the blinds, saw a man frozen to the metal of the baggage car when the tender threw water picking it up on the fly. I was on a train with ballast in my pockets. Then I said something I thought she could use. *Never get off where there is no shade.*

I meant that.

She asked me when I left school, and I told her when they started in with algebra. If X was what you didn't know, then I didn't want it.

She lost interest after that. She turned to look out the window at the orchards being sprayed.

We were heading, though she didn't know it, to Mackinac Island in the straits. It's at the top of Michigan. The road is like a life line through the state's palm. It was there we got mixed up in a troop convoy. On maneuvers, I guess. Reserve Guard. I had seen convoys in the southbound lane with their lights on, antennas bowed over on the jeeps. The trucks have a round-shouldered look, like they're hunching down the hot highway. We came up on their replacements heading north. The last vehicle was a jeep with MPs in white helmets in it. I scooted around, and then around the next deuce and a half. I blew my horn. I could see the cops shaking their heads, yelling and pointing. They weren't happy to have their string broken up. I tucked the Pontiac in between two trucks, waited for the lane to clear, then leapfrogged another truck.

I could see, when I swerved out there to pass, that the line went on for what looked like miles ahead. She perked up when we started passing. Rolled down her window. Took off her sunglasses.

As we got along deeper into the convoy, she waved to the boys. I could tell they knew right away she was a girl. Some drivers sped up to get a good look, pacing us and not letting me jog around. I could see the jeep of MPs in the rearview. It was working its way up the line behind us. They passed when we passed, eyes on us.

She yelled out to each truck. How far you going? Where you going? And then she would listen for a boy to shout how good-looking she was. I kept my eyes on the road. Listen to them, will you?

Laughing.

I felt sad seeing her reach out so far and trying to hold hands with some boy while the wind blew.

But I got to the head of the line, and that was that.

It was dark in Mackinaw City. A storm was on the lake. We could see the white in the water. Here was the end of the world as far as I was concerned. Even the roads ran out.

Across the water there was an island with no cars, restaurants that might sell my chicken. We'd take the ferry in the morning.

I arranged for a cabin. It had a small stove and a sink. I grabbed some food from a grocery just as it closed. Then I cooked dinner, using her skillet. I took my knives and started cleaning chicken, telling her I'd been cooking it since I was six. I told her about Momma peeling tomatoes all day for Stokely–Van Camp in Henryville. I told her about May apples, greens, sassafras buds. I let her help, showing her how to peel a potato, snap the skin off the garlic with the flat of the knife. She was helpless, and I asked her why she brought the pan along anyway. She had seen pictures of Johnny Appleseed when she was a kid. She was serious, she said, about leaving home. I was cutting an onion. I can cut an onion, if it is a good onion, in such a way that it stays whole for a few seconds after I am done slicing. One instant it is whole, the next a pile of a hundred pieces. She had me do this several times. You have to know what to do with it once you have it, I said, thinking of her frying pan, of the onions, well, of everything. We were both crying tears we didn't mean. We ate in silence. She said she loved the food. Everybody does.

The storm boomed on outside. I don't think she knew where she was. Not just that moment—an old log cabin with an old man—but where in the world. Maybe if she knew, she would have considered turning back. The highway was pretty slow after all. Camping with her family all over again. I looked at her as she looked at the fire and wondered if she would be telling stories about this ancient man crossing roads with chickens. She asked me what held the onion together in the first place and if I ever tried to put it all back together like a puzzle.

I slept outside in the back seat of the car. She hadn't said one thing, not one way or the other. There are certain lines I don't cross. I hadn't offered her candy, only stone soup. To me it is all the same. When my belly's full, so is the rest of me. Maybe she just didn't have the words. Outside the Pontiac, it was bad. The chief's head flashed. I went to sleep in the smell of sage and fresh ground pepper.

In the morning, it was all there. My spices, the storm, the girl in the cabin.

We drove to the ferry. But we could see from the water that no one was going anywhere. We got out and stood around. Some places you never reach.

I asked her what she wanted.

She said, "Let's just go. Just keep moving."

We headed south down 131. Nothing to talk about. No sun to give her a clue to the direction. The tin of the pressure cooker whistled as we drove.

It is the pressure cooker that is the secret. No waiting. Eight minutes to cook your goose. Didn't she know how much danger she would have been in if she hadn't been with me?

We crossed back into Indiana. Sleeping, she didn't wake up till I slowed for an Amish buggy around Nappanee. Horses and wagons were everywhere on the roads and in the fields. I got the car wheels to straddle the manure. That part of the country is the way Henryville was when I was growing up. Broad-brim straw hats and beards, suspenders and serge. Lordy, what I've seen. Now she wasn't half an hour away from where I picked her up in Fort Wayne, but she was way back in time. She was losing ground. She made me pass a wagon real slow as she stared, from behind her sunglasses, deep into the bonnet of the lady driver. She wanted to know what they were doing in the fields. Why they looked the way they looked. It was all so far away to her.

Not much farther up U.S. 6, she said here was where she would get out. All she had to do was say the word. She thanked me. I pulled over and stopped, got out and fetched her roll from the trunk. We'd parked next to a muckfield planted in peppermint. It had already been cut and raked into rows. The air reeked of it and onions in a field nearby. No shade in sight. She hadn't gotten a thing from me but a ride down the road. I told her to be careful.

I was able to look back at her a long time since the peat fields are so flat. I wondered if she realized what a difference a few feet make, that just this side of Fort Wayne is that continental divide turning the river back on its tributaries and dividing up the country as sure as the mountains out west. She probably didn't know how it all fit together. A small rise on the plain could cut her off forever. I turned a corner and never saw her again. I drove the rest of the day and night only stopping for gas.

Now it's your turn to tell me what this is all about. Who was she? Has something happened? Have I broken some law?

All the time I was with her I could see she didn't know word one about drummers or bums or bindle stiffs. But who was I to tell her? The roads are different now. But what's it to do with me? I'm glad that part of my life is behind me.

◆▸

Alfred Kinsey, Alone, after an Interview, Dreams of Indiana

I could never tell a dirty story. There is the one about the new convict and the numbered jokes, but that is not the type of thing I am thinking about. Well, anyway, the new convict calls out a number, and no one laughs because some people can't tell a joke. Pomeroy used to laugh at that one, probably more out of respect than anything else. I was, by that time, a kind of authority.

In the fall, Clara and I would borrow a car and head out of town on a Sunday. The leaves would be turning. I like the way fall works. The leaves not turning really, only the green going, and the carotene showing through for once.

We always saw it on our way to Brown County, saw a car pulled off onto the shoulder, occupants out there picnicking or napping near an overlook. And with the leaves forgetting themselves all around us, so would we. We'd try to get a look at the parkers. All this nature, but what we wanted was a look at each other. I always used this anecdote to teach my beginning classes the concept of species recognition. Interbreeding population is the last distinction before variety, I am convinced. It is the only instinct. Our heads are literally turned.

Martin kept expecting the women to lift their blouses. He was always saddened by the disparity between the public and the private history. He never doubted which was true. I remember him going over the histories of his classmates at Indiana. With the files open before him, he just sat there shaking his head. He had believed everything his friends had told him.

The first warm day and the whole department would head out to the quarries around Bloomington. Imagine, in the first days of spring, their spouses within reach again, everyone is on the lookout for the return to life of some specific fauna. All these men, knowing the oestrus of their special species, have these females next to them on crazy quilts. Our peculiar nature. Look at them. Their heads bent to the obscene buzz of zoölogy. The University spelled zoölogy with that pesky umlaut overhead. The mark the Prussians left behind after drawing out the blood. There was a white dust on all the leaves from the gypsum factories. Spring in Indiana. The cut and tumbled blocks of the abandoned quarry must have looked like ruins to a German scholar. This was a new world for me. Let them find a story here. Clara was next to me, white from the winter but already tanning. The rocks were warming up. I had just turned associate, and felt secure. So I stopped them before they could get their killing jars from the car. Yes, I stopped them by taking off my clothes and diving headlong into the pool of someone else's reflection.

We could talk shop in the most public of places because of the code. I would say, "My last history liked Y better than CM although Go in Cx made him very ez." That type of rendering made everyone more comfortable. That was during McCarthy and the Customs Case. Our books could not be sent through the mail. The Institute and the University were very sensitive. We had recently lost the Rockefeller money. No one was laughing at anything.

Clara and I, during the first hot summers in Bloomington, would walk its streets and alleys, mildly interested in the bees collecting around the backdoor rubbish bins of restaurants. Pleased when we distinguished characteristics readily. Family, order, class. The tiny mass of Latin, yellow and brown, lighted on the red bricks. Their abdomens pulsed and touched. The wasps scribbled on the surface of a pool of water. Genus, species, variety. We went to Dunn Meadow and turned the oak leaves over in our hands, recognizing the wasp by the disruption of the cells, the black gall on the dull side of the leaf. Rummaging through campus to where the Jordan River disappeared underground, we read the leaves until it was too dark to see the beauty marks, left, and grabbed a bench on Kirkwood. From there we watched the couples collect under the yellow lights of the Von Lee as they waited to buy their tickets. We saw them touch each other. We did not care who was watching us watching. Paying no attention to the miller in the light or the cricket in the dark, we rounded the corner to the Book Nook, empty and quiet between terms. The soda jerk behind the counter told us again where the speaks were that summer as he screwed his towel into the glasses while I sat down at the piano where Hoagy Carmichael had composed "Stardust" and played Chopin and Beethoven, without distinction. We closed the place, circled back to ours, and, without turning on the lights, stumbled by the sheets of insects under glass, the cotton and the chlorides, the spreading boards and pins, and, with nothing left to identify, fell in bed with the house as hot as it had been all day.

My secret was never to show surprise. I told my interviewers to assume that everyone had done everything. Anything that could be imagined is humanly possible. We had only to ascertain when and how many times.

Clara would sometimes bring my lunch down to Jordan Hall when the Institute was just setting up house. "Honey," I said to her, "this building will one day house more pornography than the Vatican." We laughed. She always understood when I was joshing. We sat on the steps where Dellenbeck liked to take our picture and watched the young men across the way strip down to the waist and knock off for lunch. The WPA was building

Sycamore and the Auditorium, and the CCC was adding a wall around the campus. Everything was done in the local limestone, which would turn from pink to gray in winter. That summer those boys with their farmer's tans molted into men. Thomas Hart Benton used some of them in the murals he did for the Auditorium. I took his history when he was on the campus. That afternoon we shared a lunch Clara brought, back in the woods where the river traced through the exposed bedrock. He wore overalls and talked about Missouri. Clara sat with her legs curled under her skirt. He stretched out his hand and touched her cheek saying, simply, "Bounty."

Pomeroy thought I derived some pleasure from keeping secrets. That was the psychologist in him talking. I never would reveal anything, of course, nor hold anything over anyone's head. It wasn't power that interested me.

I remember when Pomeroy broke my code, found and read my history, and Clara's and the children's. Of course, I was upset. But it pleased me even more that he was so willing to learn.

Her waist was gone. She was white in the moonlight. I remember, because the curtains were gone. Laundry. The baby was showing and had already moved. It was past the time we had agreed upon to do anything more. Her waist was gone, and she was a different creature. But it was summer, I remember, because I would stay up after she went to sleep and listen for insects. She had longings for cream puffs. I could keep nothing from spoiling. She could no longer move. There was no surprise. The introduction of love is its own undoing.

I told my researchers that there were only three ways a subject could not be reporting accurately. He could exaggerate, conceal, or remember imprecisely. Our methods took care of all three. The number and speed at which we ask our questions took care of most problems. No one could prepare a life, especially a sexual one, on the spur of the moment. The rest was in the follow-up, to see if the same story could be told twice.

I no longer ask myself certain questions. Donald died the year of my first *Biology*. It was Mill, I believe, who began his auto-biography with a reference to his father's book on India. Author and Father. At the Institute, we interviewed each other every year or so. I have gone through my sexual history over twenty times. I've never found the slightest inconsistency; my stories match from year to year. The repetition makes everything clearer in my mind. In others, this justifies our methodology. The story is to remain the same. I am not so sure in my own case. I have been over everything again and again, but no single night presents itself to me as the one during which Donald was conceived. *Sexual Behavior in the Human Male* took ten years to write, and I can still recite the seed of that story. I even remember what the woman wore, the pearl at her throat. Perfection out of ir-ritation. She was one of the students in the marriage course. In conference, she asked me how much passion she should expect from her fiancé. And I didn't know. Not then. Donald was three when he died. My first son. Some passion spent long ago.

I told my interviewers that some subjects would make ad-vances. I prepared them for this as best I could. I knew it would happen. I had instructed them to remain impassive, always im-passive. Nothing cools ardor more than impassivity. We did not want to lose the oral history, though. We did not want to lose anything.

There were about fifty different measurements taken on each specimen of gall wasp. And this was only morphology, not phy-logeny, host relationships, geographic distribution, life cycles and history, or gall polymorphism. I no longer had the time for the rest of it, and couldn't find a graduate student so inclined. I was caught up in the other work. By this time I had finished two books on the *Cynips*. That was enough of a contribution.

I remember watching Clara once as she measured the third segment of antennae. She would still work on the plates with water colors and go over the Leach drawings after the children were in bed. She would use the colored pencils to write me notes. I told her the new study interested me more. No more pictures to draw. "Imagine," she said, "the illuminated manuscript of this. A different box of colors." I gave the rest of the specimens to Harvard and went to the field again, collecting.

That man in the West Side bar in New York, I remember every word. "I am Dr. Kinsey, from Indiana University, and I am making a study of sexual behavior. Can I buy you a drink?" What could he say? I took his history. He was a homosexual prostitute and was so pleased that I had been telling the truth that for years after that he encouraged his friends to be interviewed. I took his history. I got it. But what impressed him more, my innocence or my knowledge?

I always hired interviewers with stable marriages. It was the nature of the work. My experience of Americans led me to believe that they were skeptical of those who cannot keep house and home together. Of course, we had to travel a great deal, we really did, and then be alone with those consenting adults in any little bit of privacy we could find. Very little was lost on us.

Clara stayed behind with the children. I left with the men, and Clara finished the pictures she had started years before of the gold bands on the abdomen of *Sphecids*.

So many people wanted to tell me things. I let them. I simply let them talk. That was what was important. Let them hear themselves. I just listened. They wanted to tell me secrets so that someone knew they kept them, that they had secrets to keep. When the study started, I, of course, interviewed myself, following my life until its history ran out. Clara's history, the one Pomeroy came across, was contrived from the things I knew. She could never tell me things. I made it all up.

There are many ways of saying yes. I have trained myself to hear them all. When I interviewed, the code we used could represent every subtlety by making each different affirmation a different word. There is even a yes that means no, of course, and the many ways of saying no. This is all I have needed to understand the lovers of the world.

Winter in Indiana. The brown oak leaves stay on the tree through the winter. The dry leaves say yes. The stones turn from pink to gray. I will die of this enlarged heart, my doctor says, because there is no time to take the rest I need.

Whistler's Father

To get to the fort, you have to cross the St. Mary's River on an arched footbridge made of concrete and steel. The bridge is steep enough to make you lean forward. There is nothing moving on the river that needs this kind of clearance.

The St. Mary's runs down under the Spy Run Bridge, and then it meets the St. Joe River, to form the Maumee, which flows on to Toledo and Lake Erie.

The fort is built on the tongue of land between the two rivers. So it floods a lot. But this summer they've lifted the rollers down on the Anthony Street Dam, and the rivers are almost dry.

I can see the Three Rivers Apartments down by the confluence from here, the elevated tracks built over the old canal, and the whole sweep of Fort Wayne's skyline—bank towers, the golden dome of the courthouse. It is the kind of picture they like to show before the local news. Along the river, I can still see some piles of sandbags from the spring's flood and the lines each crest left through the summer. The riverbed is beginning to dry and crack below the levee. I like to stand here each morning on my way to the fort and watch all the flags go up on the buildings downtown.

*   *   *   *

I work at the fort. The bridge is supposed to make it easier for the visitors to imagine they're walking into the past. You have to leave your car on the lot next to the ticket booth and cross the bridge to the fort. Spy Run, after it crosses the river, goes right by the fort, but they do it this way instead. The ticket booth is also a gift shop with little brass cannons, postcards, pens and pencils. There are racks with all the literature. At night the bridge is closed off. There is a gate made out of cyclone fencing that hangs way out over each side of the walkway so nobody can climb around it. I think it's funny, a little screen fence protecting a fort.

The oak logs of the fort are white and unweathered. They would have been unweathered then. It is always the summer of 1816.

We do all the regular things other places do—like dip candles, card wool, spin, and weave. The soldiers make shot and clean their weapons. Someone plays the fife. The children hold their ears when we shoot off the six-pounder. But we're not saying all the time, "This is how they make stew on an open fire" or "This is where the men sat and read their Bibles."

Everybody plays a person, somebody who was really here in 1816, and we make up stories to get the facts across. Otherwise, we just go about our business, answer questions when we can.

"Do you think Polk will be President?" We just look at each other and scratch our heads. "Who's he, mister?"

There are fifteen stars on the flag and fifteen stripes. They are running out of room. The Congress is trying to figure out what to do next.

When I head in the gate, Jim is working out the flogging with Marshall. There was a flogging on this day in 1816.

I am George Washington Whistler. I'll die during an epidemic in St. Petersburg, Russia, in 1849.

I was in Russia as an engineer, building the railroad between St. Petersburg and Moscow for the Czar, making harbor improvements, looking over the dockyards. One of my sons will be the painter James Abbot McNeill Whistler, who was in London when I died. He was only sixteen. That's why you never see a portrait of his father.

In the summer of 1816, I am sixteen too.

My father designed and built this fort, the third and last American fort on the site, as well as the one that was standing here in 1800. That's the fort I was born in.

Most of what I know about George is all going to happen to him after he leaves here—his marriage, his work on the border between the U.S. and Canada. That doesn't help me much now. So I just do what I think a sixteen-year-old would have done back then. I fetch things. I haul water. I whittle. I run across the compound while the soldiers drill. I tag behind Jim, who is Major John Whistler, my father, until he pretends to send me on errands. I sulk in the corner of his office while he lectures on strategy and boasts of the fort's design to a group of visitors. I gripe about school to the other kids. We've got some books from the time—primers and things. Or I tell them about how it was when we walked here from Detroit. Most of all, I talk about leaving and heading off to the military academy at West Point.

That's what's going to happen to my person pretty soon, and that's most of what I know, things that will happen soon.

Late in the day, with my chores all done, I'll go down to the river and skip a few stones. The people crossing back over the bridge will be able to see me there on the bank.

Most of the other people who work here—the soldiers and their wives, the settlers, the traders—are history majors out at Indiana–Purdue University on the bypass. They are always telling me a new fact they've come up with in the library—like a diary that mentions something a person did, or what was in a letter found folded in an old book. They're always building things up from just a few clues. My sister, Harriet, for instance, is supposed to have been a real gossip and mean. That's what they decided from some letters they found along with a recipe for cornbread. She fretted greatly over Major Whistler, our father, who seems to have not gotten along at all with B. F. Stickney, the Indian agent, or with his son-in-law, Lieutenant Curtis. I've seen Jim— who is really a professor out at the campus—have yelling matches with the man who plays Mr. Stickney. Visitors will come through the gate, and the two of them will be shouting. Major Whistler is out on the balcony of his quarters. Mr. Stickney is over by the hospital. It's something about the payments and the sale of alcohol.

Nobody tells the visitors what they're getting into. They just have to catch on. It must seem like these are real fights at first.

The visitors move around, trying to get out of the way, and I ignore the whole thing. So we're pretending all the time, and as the summer's gone on, the little things we've started with have been added to.

It takes all day to do everything we've invented to do.

One soldier shoves me up against the flagpole every morning to show how nasty he was supposed to have been. Someone else does nothing but stay in bed in the hospital. He dies all summer. But he's been gaining weight.

We are always saying how we could really use people who can speak French the way they did back then.

This is educational for everybody. The fathers are always quieting their sons saying, "Listen to this," as the Sergeant Major pats the barrel of the howitzer and tells his little story about Fallen Timbers. The women and the girls hang around the kitchens and out near the bower down by the river, where the ladies from the fort do the laundry. Sometimes people will help weed the plots of vegetables or churn butter. They'll add a few stitches to the quilt.

The college kids who work here get credit, I think. Or write papers. Something.

Everybody who visits is interested in sanitation.

I take people around to the privies, point out the chamber pots, tell them how it was a real problem in the previous fort during the war and the siege.

"Here is the gutter that Major Whistler, my father, had dug around the parade ground for the water to run off."

I've learned a lot too about history and speaking in front of people. I like talking about these things and having people listening. I like it when they nod and whisper to each other. The little boys look at what I'm wearing.

Kids my age will try to trip me up, asking about hamburgers or the Civil War. But I haven't made a mistake once. Well, once I did, but the guy who asked didn't know I did, so it was all right.

I'll be a senior next year at North Side High School, which is up on the banks of the St. Joe near the site of a French fort. Fifty years ago, when they dug the foundation, they found an Indian burial site. That's why we're called the Redskins. My teachers think this will be good experience. They wrote good recommendations for me. My own father isn't so sure, but he is happy I have a job and that I work outside.

To him, it's a summer job, that's all.

Lieutenant Curtis, who is my brother-in-law by marriage to my sister Eliza, has mustered the garrison together for the morning assembly and flag raising. The orders and officers of the day are posted, regulations concerning fraternization and venereal disease are read. He goes on a bit about B. F. Stickney, thinking aloud about the man's character. The men are at parade rest. They're dressed in the hot wool uniforms or the white fatigues.

The flag is popping.

There is already a large crowd watching.

Behind the crowd is a file of late arrivals going in and out of the buildings.

Before we opened, we talked about fudging a bit, holding up the flogging until we had enough people to make it worthwhile. That won't be a problem now. It's something we always have to work out since the visitors aren't around for the whole day usually. We don't want anyone to go away without seeing a special event, a rifle firing or the band playing at least. But we can't be flogging every hour on the hour.

"Next flogging in twenty minutes."

We try to be true to the facts we have. The trouble is that the visitors see a few hours of what took years to come about. So it's kind of hard to explain why they're whipping this man today. It's funny that more people don't ask.

It is all done by the book—down to the knots and the tattoo the drummer's doing. I am sitting on the roof of the magazine. The magazine is the shed where they kept the powder and munitions. It was supposed to be brick, so it wouldn't burn or blow up. But there were just too many trees around. Major Whistler sodded the roof instead, and the grass is long and green.

The magazine is near the east wall. Between the *thwap, thwap* of the whip and Marshall's screaming, I can hear the traffic going by on Spy Run.

The street is on the other side of the wall. Cars honk at the sentry in the blockhouse from time to time as they go by.

The real fort was on the other side of the river, near where the apartments are now, up on the high ground. That's how they got the land to build this fort. It's on the flood plain along with all the parks.

There is a lot of flood plain when you have three rivers running through a town.

One of the first jobs I did in the spring was sandbag the fort during the flood. We pumped the water out into Spy Run and back into the river. But the water really didn't go anywhere. I was happy to work three days and nights without pay. It was a good way to get to know the people I was going to work with.

And it was a big flood, a hundred-year flood, and I was in it with historians.

That night the President's helicopter was beating around overhead. Its spotlight was dancing all around and lighting up this little clearing. There we were, passing heavy wet bags. The water was rippling into waves from the rotors. Looking up I could see the rain pouring through the beam of light. Jim still worries about rot damage to the wood, termites and such, but everything is green and cool this summer, and it will probably stay this way until fall.

The roof is nice with clover blooming.

Most of the people in the crowd wear dark glasses. We can't, of course. My face is tired at night from squinting. I have just started wearing contacts, so I can go without my glasses. Jim's face is lined from the weather and from worry. We're always trying to get the visitors to see how much quicker people aged then.

This will be my only summer here, you know. George Washington Whistler has to be sixteen.

Marshall's been carried off to the hospital. Lieutenant Curtis has dismissed the men, and they are dispersing. My sisters have been dabbing the corners of their eyes with handkerchiefs. Their bonnets hide a part of their faces. My father is talking to a group of visitors, slapping his gloves, in his hand, on his flexed knee— talking about discipline and justice and a peacetime army, I imagine.

"Who are you?" says a little boy, calling up to me on the magazine roof.

He is wearing sunglasses with six-shooters in the upper corners of the lenses.

I tell him who I am, and he asks if I know the soldier who was beaten.

I tell him that I do know him and why he was punished.

"Can I come up there?" the boy asks.

"Nope," I say.

This isn't the only thing I've been doing this summer. I still go out. I ride around town with some of the guys from school. We make the loop from the one Azar's Big Boy out on the bypass to the other one by South Side High School. Everybody's got their first jobs, running registers or dropping fries. They cut grass on Forest Park. It gives them money for the cars and enough left over to order food and hold down a booth without getting kicked out.

Some of my friends are going to summer school, and that's what my job seems like to the others, like summer school.

We go by the Calvary Temple sign that flashes *Calvary, Temple, Calvary, Temple.*

Clinton splits off into a one-way street. We go past the old power plant and the fenced substation with wires going out everywhere. On the ribs of the big transformers are these fans pointed at the fins on the side. They are on sometimes to cool down the transformers. But at night the blades are feathering, turning slowly in the breeze.

Les always says how funny it is that they use some electricity to run the fans to cool the transformers to make the electricity. Over the St. Mary's, by the armory, under the overpass, through downtown, under the overpass, and into the near south side of the city. Coming back, we go up Lafayette, which turns into Spy Run by the bridge. We go by the fort, all dark of course, except for the lights of the cars playing along the walls, and the guys all kid me. One night, they'll break in, and it will be trouble for me. Maybe T. P. the whole place. They'll leave my name in red paint on the walls.

We head north by Penguin Point, with the trash cans shaped like penguins, and then run along the bike path on the bank of the St. Joe. We cross State and off to the right is North Side across the river. The ventilating scoops all swiveling like weather vanes left and right. That's another thing we can never figure out, how those scoops are all pointed in different directions in the same breeze. Spy Run bears down on the Old Crown Brewery, dead ahead, but turns sharp left to meet up again with Clinton. Mr. Centlivre is all lit up on the building's roof. His foot is planted on a keg like a big game hunter. We start talking about going to Ohio. But we never do.

On weeknights I keep score for my dad's softball team. I fill up the frames with little red diamonds. They're winners. It's fast pitch. They have uniforms and everything. When the ball gets by the catcher and no one's on base, he throws it to the third baseman, who always plays in. The third baseman relays it back to the pitcher, a windmiller, his ball jumping over the plate. They're sharp. I call out the lineups. On deck, in the hole.

They all ask about the fort and tell me how they mean to come by.

They work during the day, and on vacation they usually go away. I tell them there is plenty to see right here in town. But they know I am kidding.

I like the plinking sound of the aluminum bats. I like to see the white ball go bouncing beyond the lights out into the high grass of Hamilton Park, a grown man chasing after it like a kid.

I warm Dad up before the game, taking one step back after two throws. He's always very deliberate, pretending to throw after he throws. He tells himself what he's doing wrong. I can hear snatches of it. I'm all encouragements. When he's not in the field but swinging the lead bat, I hold his glove to keep it off the ground, make sure there's a ball inside to keep the pocket.

Dad takes some of us from the fort to the various parades and festivals where we've been appearing. We go all over this part of Indiana. Mom comes along to help with the maps and to look over the handicrafts. They won't accept mileage. We're all in the backseats of the station wagon in full-dress uniforms. Shakos, crossing white belts, bayonets in the scabbards. The muskets are up on the luggage rack. Mom always says, "I bet the wool is itchy."

We don't look very smart since our clothes are authentic and handmade. You'd expect more. But we do all right in the parades, staying in step and following orders. We fire off a salute at least once.

Dad works for Rea Magnet Wire and worries about the way the car smells. As long as I can remember, his cars have smelled of copper and the enamels. He even smells that way when I get close enough to him. It's like something you were trying to melt in a pan, chocolate or butter, was just starting to burn instead.

He hangs little green paper Christmas trees from the rearview mirror, but they don't do any good. Mom asks why draw attention to it by trying to cover it up. I don't think the people from the fort notice—or if they do, they get used to it like we all do. They're nervous about the parade and how they look.

All summer I have been thinking about my chemistry problem. I'll be taking third-year chem in the fall. I've liked chem since the first class. It's the teacher, I think, and because I have a knack for it. My senior year will be organic and a special project. I've known what I wanted to do for a long time, ever since Mr. Dvorak showed us the clock reaction in an early lecture.

A clock reaction is close to magic.

The stuff in the beaker changes colors all by itself.

It didn't seem like science at all. That's why it was great for beginning classes. He poured these three clear liquids into a beaker. The liquid turned a bright orange and seemed to thicken. He kept on stirring slowly with a glass rod, clinking it against the glass beaker. All of a sudden, the orange turned black. It was just like someone had flicked a switch. He told us that a professor at Princeton had designed the reaction, and that orange and black are the Princeton colors.

Since then, I've been thinking about my own clock reaction in white and red, North Side High colors. It has to be in that order since the white couldn't cover the red.

I need to find three compounds, ABC. A and B can't react. B and C can't react. But A and C do react, and their product is a white solid. In that product somewhere there has to be something that will then combine with B, but not all at once.

I can't have pink.

For two years I've been mixing precipitates—blue-green coppers, orange potassiums, cobalt blues, the yellows. The test tubes go from clear to color, and the solid settles instantly or suspends, milky and in motion.

Iron gives red, and there are many white metals.

Dvorak says there are tables and books that just list the colors. That would save me time, but I like to see them for myself— the colors and the grades of solids, sand or silt or crystal. There's one, just a drop, that turns as it falls through the acid, a little gray worm by the time it hits the bottom.

Don't worry—one day I'll say, "See?"

White, red.

My mother thinks I think too much. She's caught me staring into the sink, watching the Ajax oxidate and turn blue. She thinks I should go out more. My dad doesn't say anything but worries out of habit. We'll sit together out on the porch swing. I'll be reading, and he'll be smoking a cigar. "Boats this year," he'll say after a while. "Sailboats."

He's thinking about the Junior Achievement projects for next fall.

Rea gives copper wire to a J A company.

The kids make pictures of things by stringing the wire between carefully arranged pegs. Cars, trains, airplanes—all made out of thread-gauge copper wire, gold-headed tacks, black cloth for the background.

I am waving to the Kiwanis pontoon going by on the river. I can hear pieces of the talk about the beautification project, the downtown, the fort, the portage that made this spot worth fighting for in the first place. My two sisters are washing nearby, letting the crowd of visitors overhear them talk about the Major, our father, and finding him a wife, how that would make him more tolerable to live with. I go on back to the clearing in front of the gate where the rifle squad is drilling and the cannon is being readied for firing. The visitors shade their eyes, take pictures.

They've been blowing up buildings across the river downtown. It's the easiest way to demolish the vacant old hotels. From here, we can see some of it. A building turns to dust and disappears from between the other buildings. If the wind is right, there is hardly any sound, just the cloud of dust rolling away. The Keenan Hotel. The Van Ormen. Once the gun crew tried to time a firing with one of the explosions. They aimed the cannon in the general direction so it would look like we were shelling the downtown, the building collapsing before our guns. Jim said it was a stupid idea. The visitors were more interested in the drill, swabbing out the barrel, ramming, loading, the slow-burning fuse. The visitors were from out of town anyway and probably didn't know what was going on. The local people would be downtown to watch the building go.

The problem is that it is so hard to imagine this place without buildings even though so much of the old city is leveled now into fields of rubble. The view is broken only by the steeples of the old German churches.

It's easy for me to pretend I've never tasted white sugar. Basketball hasn't been invented. But I think I stick too close to the facts. Maybe I can't see much beyond the things I can see.

My friend Les isn't like that at all. He told me once of the project he'd like to do. Since energy is just matter traveling at the speed of light, he told me, what he'd like to come up with would be some kind of filter that would slow things down. Hold it up to the light and solid blocks of stuff would fall out of the air.

"That would be better than your clock reaction," he says. "You might have to pick stuff up, but you wouldn't have the mess afterwards."

And Jim has no trouble at all being someone else. It is 1816 to him. "Listen," he says, "what bird did that? One of the swallows from the blockhouse?"

He's proud of the fort's innovations—the cubiles for putting out fires, the overhanging ports to shoot down on intruders crouching by the walls. He's proud that he's convinced the banks to see it all like he saw it and that he convinced the city fathers to go along. There are signs all over town pointing in this direction. *See Old Fort Wayne.* For the longest time, all there was of the fort was one replica cannon in the lobby of the library, flanked by a glass case with a model made out of toothpicks and paper.

It had been there as long as I could remember.

It is late in the day. The pies that Harriet and Eliza made are in the windows. I'm supposed to swipe one and take it off to the soldier's mess. The sisters search each building, rolling pin at the ready. But the men hide me from my sisters. The visitors scream with laughter as I race from one building to another a step ahead of my pursuers. The visitors are on all the porches, resting on the hand-hewn chairs and benches. The sun is hot. The sky is blue. I make it to the hospital and disappear inside just as the sisters emerge from the southeast blockhouse.

Major Whistler steps out on the porch of his quarters and shouts with command, "What in God's name is going on here!"

The sisters confide to those nearby that the boy needs a mother, that he's getting too big to chase after.

Harriet is portrayed as a flirt, though distracted with the care of her father. Her motivation for wishing to see our father married again comes from her own desire to be free to find a husband. She will later marry a Captain Phelan who will be killed in Detroit. She'll live to 1872. Harriet.

Major Whistler will become the military storekeeper at Bellefontaine, Missouri. He will move with the troops to the new Jefferson Barracks in 1826, and die there in September.

Eliza will go with her husband, Lieutenant Curtis, from here to Detroit to Green Bay. She will have a child in the cradle and one in school when, one day, while washing clothes in a river near Fort Howard, she will be killed by a bolt of lightning. That's it for Eliza.

Daniel Curtis and I are eating pieces of pie in the hospital. He is there caring for Marshall. The record shows that Curtis served as the fort doctor that summer when there was no one else to do it. Had some training, had some schooling. He was liked by the Indians, having witnessed the speeches at Brownstown in 1810. He was a schoolteacher from New Hampshire.

"Stickney," he said, "is an opportunist. He is receiving money from the whiskey-traders."

The pie is very good. Made with berries from our own canes.

It is hard for me to keep from thinking about the futures of these people. I feel sorry for Curtis, though it is years before his wife's death and his bungling at Fort Howard. He will be court-martialed and discharged.

We sit and eat the warm pie in pieces he's cut with his knife. We've hidden what's left of it beneath a bunk. The man who plays Curtis winks at me a lot.

The visitors stick their heads in the door. They see us eating the pie in what seems a normal fashion. They see another log building, bare and chinked. The planking has been ripped out by a two-man saw. The only color is the leather fire bucket in the corner. It's painted blue.

Les says that it would drive him crazy.

"It's enough for me just to not think about school this fall."

We are sitting on the riverbank by North Side, down below the concrete levee. The brewery makes the air smell rotten.

Cottonwood seeds are floating in the green water. I tell him it's kind of like living with premonitions all the time or ESP.

"It's neat knowing everything," I say.

The clock on the brewery has read twenty after ten since it was sold to a national brewer.

"See," I say, "they're going to let that place go right down the drain. Let it all just fall apart."

Les just grunts and heaves a rock to make the pigeons fly. Cadmium is light blue, I think, and rhodium is red but expensive. Iodine is not really black but violet. A dark violet.

We have been spying on the cheerleaders who are practicing in the parking lot by the school. We watch them from behind the levee as they work on their movements. The way they clap their hands and bounce on their toes. They climb on each other's knees and backs. They do the type of cheers you like to watch even though you can't cheer along with them. Splits and flips. They wear red sweatshirts, white skirts.

"Try and explain that to future generations," Les says. We keep watching through the afternoon, ducking down to the river when we think they've seen us. The littlest one is on the top of the pyramid. We see her skirt fly up. She lands on her feet and bounces. Falling with her from all over the formation are the other girls, landing and clapping. They bounce, no longer in unison. Applaud what they've done. Then they do the pyramid cheer again.

I like to think the painter Whistler didn't paint a picture of his father because he was like me. He didn't trust his memory, was only comfortable with a model sitting in front of him. He was my age when his father died, and he'd just started drawing.

I have a collection of postcards with reproductions of his paintings and his etchings. Les says if I have etchings, I should tell the cheerleaders to come around and take a look.

They are pictures of docks and streets in France and England—highly detailed—panes in the windows and reflections in the glass. The portraits are all very sad, though I can see that they are beautiful. They are titled after their colors and compared to music.

Arrangement in Black and White.

Blue Nocturnes.

Things like that.

The picture of his mother has a picture hanging on the wall that I can barely make out. I think it is another one of his pictures. I can't imagine what he looked like. George, I mean. Sideburns, I guess. A high collar? The Czar took a ruler and drew a straight line from St. Petersburg to Moscow.

"Do this," he said.

And Whistler did.

His father, Major Whistler, and B. F. Stickney are having it out near the gate. Everyone draws in, the garrison as well as the remaining visitors, who feel better about what is happening around them now. This is all made up, they are thinking.

"How dare you, sir! How dare you!" Stickney is saying.

The Major produces maps and indicates lands deeded by the treaty of Greenville to the Richardville clan of the Miami in perpetuity.

"There are white settlers on the land, Mr. Stickney. Here and here."

I see my father in the crowd, listening to what's going on.

I guess it looks like a dispute at home plate, both benches emptied.

Soldiers are moving in with muskets. They begin breaking through the crowd. Lieutenant Curtis holds the two men apart. His hat is knocked off his head. "Gentlemen! Gentlemen!"

I edge over to my father, who asks me what's going on. I tell him about what Stickney's been up to, selling land to families up from Kentucky, paying off the tribes, and getting the money back by tripling the whiskey prices on payment day.

I can smell the copper.

He has just come from the plant, so it's strong and mixed in with my own smell and the smell of the wool uniforms that only get washed once a week since that was regulation. My dad begins to ask me another question, but then I can see he starts to understand the way things work. So he waits for me to speak first.

He probably stopped by to give me a ride home, probably got across the bridge without paying since it's close to closing.

My eyes are very tired and I can't wait to take them out. I mean the contacts. I don't think I'll ever be able to wear them as long as they say you're supposed to.

The soldiers are pushing us all back with their muskets now. The braid on their shakos is loose. There is an eagle and a white cockade. The hats make the soldiers look taller.

My father takes a few steps back. His tie is loose but still knotted.

This is the first time he has seen the fort. I point out the gardens and the pickets and the Pennsylvania key, notched in the corners of the buildings. Cars are going by on Spy Run. Flashes of color. Engines are revved high. People are on their way home from work. We stand there on the edge of the crowd, my dad and I, listening to an argument that was settled a long time ago.

◆→

Dear John

.

I am living in Indianapolis now. Like me, it has no reason for being here. The people of the state simply wanted their capital in the middle of Indiana, paced off the distance, and brought an apprentice of L'Enfant out from Washington, D.C., to make all the same mistakes in this city's plans. Streets, named after states, radiate from circles where monumental statuary bases are waiting for statues, waiting for someone to become famous enough to become a statue. Everywhere you look in this city you see these flat-topped pyramids, empty niches in building facades, friezes without faces, metopes without bas-relief. The circles here, too, were planned for defense purposes as if someone would wish to take a thing that was never meant to be. The theory was that batteries positioned in the circles could command three hundred and sixty degrees of the neighborhood. The airplane makes this all silly, of course. But, on the other hand, it is only from the air that you can see the plan, gain any perspective on the order here. Instead, the circles cause traffic jams, rotaries coursing with cars at all hours (late-model plum-colored Chevrolets, it seems, are everywhere), all looking for numbered streets. There are quadrant designations too—NW, SE. It is very much like an army camp, except there are no white rocks. There are boulders on people's lawns. Blank bronze plaques are bolted on the sides of the boulders. In the summer, you can watch the husbands trim the grass by crawling on all fours around the boulders using those hand clippers. The boulders came all the way from Canada, their sides worn smooth for the plaques by the glaciers that carried them down here.

I came here looking for you. You're not dead yet, officially. Still listed as missing in action on the Lunghai Railroad en route to Hsuchow, China, 25 August 1945. I can't go back there now and look for you myself. What were you doing in Anhwei Province? Another airfield in the middle of nowhere? I thought when you left Changsha for the last time you were on your way to Shantung Province to organize the North. I can't remember what you said to me.

The woman at the American Legion headquarters here is very kind and helpful. She tells me that I mustn't worry, that GIs are marching home all the time. Some have knocks on the head and have lost their memories. Pockets of Japanese resistance are still being turned up on nameless atolls a dozen years after the surrender. There are prisoner exchanges all the time. Priests stumbling out of the jungle. I have pretty much given up hope, though. I go on out of habit. I think you can *keep* someone alive. I keep. I still write often to your sister Betty on the farm in Macon. I tell her about her brother in China. She tells me about growing up with you in Georgia. The farm, she writes, has now been all planted with trees, just as you wanted it to be. Elm (though there is a new disease here in the States that is killing them), tulip, white pine, and, of course, birches that do not grow well since they are not native to the South. Your father still preaches. Your mother still plays the organ for him. Things would not be that different if you came back now.

I sit in the study room at the American Legion with the other women—widows mostly, though some are old girl friends like me. We all have our files, the accordion type, filled with letters from comrades, maps, commendations, canceled orders. We wait for records to become declassified, for belongings or effects or last remains to appear from the warehouse searches in Kansas City. The older women wear hats with veils. The cross-hatch of the netting makes their faces look made up out of dots like newspaper photos. They remove just the one white glove, the one from their writing hand. The other glove is specked with the crumbs from their erasures. When a regular gives up her place by the window, someone new comes to take it and stays until, a few weeks or years later, her work too is done.

In front of the American Legion Headquarters building, a mall begins, and from there it stretches four blocks along Meridian and Pennsylvania to the Post Office. There are plazas and parks. There is a hundred-foot obelisk of black Berwick granite. Around the base is a varicolored electric-lighted water fountain. There is a cenotaph, gold Roman eagles and all. Halfway down the mall is the War Memorial, a replica one-third the size of the mausoleum erected by Artemisia. There is even a light on the plateau of the stepped roof that represents the eternal flame. Scaffolds, like the ones window-washers use, hang high up along the west wall of the building. Workmen are still carving the names of the Korean dead. Watching them, I hear the sound of hammer and chisel long after I see the blow. All of the buildings around the mall are made from limestone in that New Deal style. The U's are carved as V's. There is, on the part of the mall that begins in front of the Legion building, a vast vehicle park and ordnance dump the Legion supervises and maintains. Rows of 37mm antitank guns, howitzers (all spiked, the breechblocks gone), files of quad .50 mounts and Bofors guns. There are a few old Shermans and Grants, even a Stuart, destined for a park somewhere or maybe to be cemented in a town square. The Legion distributes the surplus to the local posts, to be set up on stoops and front lawns next to lighted flagpoles. The guns will be trained on the part of Main Street that is most menacing. Every city will have one. They can't all be hammered into plow-shares. I can imagine a crew of drunken legionnaires scrambling from a stag, manning this fieldpiece, pretending they are walking shells toward the grain elevators. In purple fatigue caps sagging with medals, these men will crank the elevation wheel because that is the only thing that is left working, and then they'll lob a few shells toward home, the wife, the kids.

After a day of looking for you, I walk along the rows of weapons, and if the wind is right, I hear the whistle coming from the vents of the air-cooled barrels. I smoke a cigarette, watch them carve the names. It is all drab and battleship gray. Everything that is loose has been stolen. There are chalk marks on the shields and fenders. Stars glow on the armor.

I live in Chinatown here. It is on the near south side in the shadow of the Lilly pill plants. To get there, I walk around the monument circle at Market Street and cross the Crossroads of America at Washington and Meridian. Under the railroad overpass. By John's Hot Stew. I don't know why I am writing this as if you will come looking for me.

Chinatown here is the type of thing you would expect. Chop suey joints above laundries or laundries above chop suey joints. Banners hang above the street. The smells of soy and dry-roasted peanuts. Taiwanese mainly. Many from the fall of the Tachen Islands. Quemoy is being shelled again. There are animated arguments at the walls where the language dailies are posted. Children dribble basketballs along the sidewalk. Wearing scarlet, they weave around their fathers. The public phones are in pagodas. The shelter signs are in Chinese.

It is not really like Changsha, though there is a jinriksha. Most people here wear black sneakers. They miss China. I can pretend I am still there—bow to the men in sleeveless shirts and gray pants in my building, share silk thread with their wives, who sew all day. I can imagine when I leave in the morning, I am on my way to the Yale-in-China Hospital again. Taste tea in a coffee cup. And I wait for you. At night in bed, I hear a train slam into the station. It is the Japanese shelling.

There is a man here who says he remembers you when you

preached in Chekiang Province. He is still a Christian and insists I go to church with him, an A.M.E. in the next ward. He says he was told you joined the AVG, that all China has heard of you. He tells me your Chinese is perfect. He would not be surprised if you were still alive and preaching to many converts. Mao himself would not be able to tell you were American. I think the man says what he thinks I want to hear; he brings me fried bananas and takes me uptown on the bus to the cathedral to play Bingo.

There is one bathroom on my floor in my building. I like to sit there, steaming in the tub. I can smell the starch from the street. Do you remember the P-40 shot down over Lingchuan when we lived there? It crashed, pilotless, down the road. I remember when the Chinese peasants, hundreds of them it seemed to me, carried the cracked-up plane up the road to our house. The smaller parts, they held them above their heads. It looked as if it was coming apart as it moved. It was like the dragons at New Year's. "Here is your plane," they shouted, dropping it near the porch. We were the only Americans they knew of. You thanked them in your perfect Chinese. Sly General Wang took the aluminum from the fuselage and had his smith make the bathtub. Remember the bathtub? All we had before was the Yangtze Kiang. The way I washed your back like an Asian wife. Why did you leave with Drummond without saying anything? You wrote to Betty trying to explain. She has shown me the letters. And you wrote to your parents. In Lingchuan, in Changsha, when we made love, you whispered to me in Chinese. In *Chinese*. I didn't know Chinese. I don't know it. The geese flying backwards. The Eastern menagerie. And I would have gone with you to the West, to Turkestan if you had wanted. Converted the Jews. It *is* a place for a woman. "Look, I have a mission." Now, *I* have a mission, John. I had one then and they are the same. You, John. Did you, in doing your duty (and was it duty to God or to country that allowed you to leave me?), confuse your two missions? A missionary is always the best warrior. I remember the Jesuits saying mass along the road in camouflage, the host made of spinach flour. I remember the almond eyes of that Flying Tiger. I kept them above our bed after you left. I would stare back at them as they bore down on me and try to imagine its smile.

I asked for you at HQ. I waited for your letters every day at the Yale Hospital. I rode my bike back home past the quilted soldiers who eyed me along the road as they unwrapped their puttees at night, just as they had wrapped them as I went to work in the morning. Your letters never came. I always left forwarding addresses. Mailed a packet of letters to your family. I tried to write the letter that would free me. I could live with the secrets of the war you shared with me. I could have lived with you and your God and your other women. I watched you for hours as you studied the code books. A mission makes us the thing we pursue. We are what we study. I am becoming you, John. Losing me. Losing us. Losing the very reason I went looking in the first place. The way you lost yourself in a China you believed could be converted into Georgia. Why did you leave me? Was it that you could no longer understand English? Had you only the taste for the cheapest red rice?

You don't know about television. Imagine one of your radios but this one sends pictures along with the words. After my bath, if the night is warm, I go down to the appliance store and watch the televisions in the window. No one in Chinatown can afford one yet. So, people come out and they watch with me. The men wear straw hats and bob up and down to see over shoulders. The women sit on the curb or lean against the few cars and listen to the man who translates the words which come from the small speaker tucked up under the awning with the sparrows' nests. There are twenty sets on tiers all tuned to the same picture. You can watch people making sure that all the pictures are doing the same thing at the same time. You can see their heads jerk from screen to screen. I go there to watch them watch. During the day, the screens are turned off, and no one stops on the sidewalk. The televisions are watching us. "Take one home," the appliance man tells me as I pass his door. "It will keep you company." He says I will never be lonely. "Come back tonight. They will all be turned on tonight."

Then I go back to the American Legion and search for you. In my file is a new commendation from Chennault. I answer mail. Write letters. Make notes in the margins of radio traffic logs.

I do not know how many letters this makes to you. For a while after the Arbor Day I spent in Georgia, I would send them to your sister there. She would write back as you. She had practiced your hand from the letters she had from you during the war, tracing them as she grew up the way other children trace animals or flowers out of encyclopedias. We both went a long way toward believing. She cut short her hair and nails, carved our initials, yours and mine, into one of the trees. She had her picture taken by the tree while she wore your old work clothes. But the closer she got to you, the more I missed the things that she was not. Maybe I am cursed with too much memory. Maybe I write these letters as a way of forgetting. I watch the nicotine stains on my fingernails grow out as the nail grows out, and I think to myself that by the time the yellow splotches reach the tip, I will be over this. They do and I am not and I smoke more and my nails are stained. Perhaps I will clip them and send them off with this letter.

Of course, there are other men. Mr. Lee, who brings me the fried bananas and the fortune cookies without fortunes he buys half-priced at the bakery thrift shop. There's him. He clips articles for me from the *National Geographic*. He takes me to movies at the Circle Theatre. There is the floorwalker at L. S. Ayres, who began by suspecting me as I wandered around the mezzanine near the stamp corner. But I was innocent, and he led me to the perfume counter where he spotted my arms with samples. What could they say to me? "He is dead and gone." They are too polite for that. To them, I am a story they could tell their grandchildren. "I knew a woman once . . . "

*   *   *   *

Recently, I met another man.

At my table at the Legion, I found a box of chocolate-covered cherries. I thought someone had forgotten them from the day before, and I tried to turn them in to the woman at the desk. She said no, they were for me. "A Mr. Welch left them for you himself." Welch's was the brand name on the box.

That night as I watched television, he appeared in the jinriksha, bedecked with flowers. "Audrey, my dear, come for a ride with me."

The men watching television looked to see him too, a tall man in a linen suit and Panama. "I am Robert Welch," he said. "It was I who left the bonbons for you." The women in the gutter clucked. "Come here," he said, "I have things to tell you about your Captain Birch." Such a nice smile. He held out a candied egg. "For you."

The men had turned back to the television in the window. The women leaned together. "I have irrefutable proof that John Birch was killed by Communists in nineteen forty-five."

Mr. Lee said, "What gives, Pops? Can't the lady watch TV in peace?"

The man said, "The meter's running, Audrey. Please, come with me. We can talk. I have been looking for you these last five years. I have good news of John Birch."

"You told me he was dead," I said.

Mr. Lee said, "Scram. Beat it, Pops." Now everyone was watching the scene in the street. The men who had been nearest the store were now in back, looking for an opening to see. Mr. Lee, sensing he was now the center of attention, continued to yell. I thanked Mr. Lee, apologized to the television audience, and got into the seat next to Mr. Welch. As we left Chinatown, the children in pajamas ran after us collecting the stray blossoms that fell from the jinriksha.

What else could I do? Another lead to track down. Such a

gentle man who had given me candy, your name. I suppose that Mr. Welch, Robert, had thought I would be grateful for the truth. The truth was that the truth didn't interest me as much as a convincing lie. Later, I found out that that was his mission, truth telling. Another truth not yours, John. He believed all he had to do was tell people the truth and they would act accordingly. Not that easy.

As we clopped around and around the monument circle he told me some more truth.

This is what the man said. He said he had made his fortune in candy and then sold the business to Nabisco. He said he spent his time and money studying the spread of Communism, that he kept a little scorecard in his wallet. He knew the political positions of Ghana and Kwame Nkrumah. He said he came across your name when you helped Doolittle, and that, as he pieced together your life in China, he turned up my name. My first name. Our affair. Our engagement. The mystery of your leaving. Now, as he looked for Communists, he also looked for me. He said he'd found, in your life and death, the ordeal of an age.

"What was he like, really?" This is what he asked.

I was eating the candied egg. I told him what he wanted to hear. A truth teller always has such simple notions of truth. I said, "A pious man. Deeply religious. His soldier's shell temporarily assumed. A gentleman. A happy warrior. Cheerful. A tinkerer. A lover of children. All the things you would expect from a man descended from a *Mayflower* Pilgrim and related, through blood, to four U.S. presidents."

I did not tell him about the rice paper, your calligraphy. The way you squatted against the wall of the hut. The bathtub.

He gave me his handkerchief to wipe the caramel from my hands. When I offered to give it back, he told me to keep it. We returned to my building and he walked me to the door.

He said, "Audrey, I must continue to see you. It is important to the Free World. You, who knew and loved John Birch, can understand what he and we should stand for."

"Yes, of course," I said.

*　　*　　*　　*

Robert took me to the 500 after we had spent the weekends in May at the time trials. We sat in the infield while the cars shot around the track. Before the race, he led a prayer for the war dead, cried when they played "On the Banks of the Wabash." He took me to restaurants. He praised you over John's Hot Stew. We went to Indian baseball games, to the state fair. The judge slapped the rump of a steer. He said, "A farmer, that's all John ever wanted to be."

Always at my desk, I would find some type of kiss. I could not concentrate on your file. All the women seemed to be weeping more than usual.

I smoked more cigarettes and bought Hershey bars from the stand in the lobby of the building. In all the public buildings, the Marion County Association for the Blind run the concession. They say they know by touch the denomination of the bill. They make change easily. They sit, their creamy eyes floating in their heads, surrounded by candy. No matter how quiet I am. "Yes, may I help you?"

I buy some gum and return to my place. I write letters to the floorwalker. I tell him I did steal some stamps. "I'll never be able to see you again." Also a letter to Mr. Lee, breaking it to him gently.

One night Robert took me to his room at the Fox Hotel. French windows led out to the balcony where he had set up a white telescope. Ten stories up you could see down to the spokes of the lighted streets as they radiated from their circles. The circles were phosphorescent craters. All along the mall, the government buildings were flooded with lights. Car lots on the south side were having sales. Surplus spotlight beams waved back and forth. I looked at the city and saw if for the first time. Robert, through his telescope, searched for Sputnik.

"There, there! That's it!" He was so happy. "Look at it as it goes by."

The stars are different in Indianapolis. I can see no dragons, no bears, no crabs. My eyes came back down to the red neon of the insurance companies on Meridian.

I am sitting here now in my usual place writing you another letter. I can't say things right. I cannot wait any longer. And, now, I am here at the signature, the farewell. Who is the John of this Dear John letter? I imagine you somewhere at mail call. The names of the dead shouted out, packages passed along on fingertips. Envelopes thrown, arms reaching out. "Yo! Here! That's me!"

What should I do? Robert will soon ask me to marry him. We will honeymoon in England, the better to study the evils of Socialism. He will read to me from newspapers over breakfast. We will talk about you as would a father and a sister. He will ask me to marry him as I walk out of this building for the last time having left a box of chocolates for the kind woman at the desk. I will wear white gloves and inspect the equipment on the lawn in front of the building. The gun barrels crisscross above our heads. The grass has grown up around the tires of the caissons and the tracks of the tanks.

Robert has shown me a picture of your funeral in Hsuchow. I have it here. I will send it to you. The Japanese probably wonder how they got into this. They want to go home now that the war is over. They look over Drummond's shoulder at the casket. The Chinese, in their German-looking helmets, are drawn up in a row, bayonets fixed but sheathed. They go out of focus as they approach the camera. There are too many stripes on the flag. Is this hope? Is it just me? The one flaw that gives the deception away. The foliage looks flat, a painted flat. The whole thing staged, a postcard from a wax museum. Why was the picture taken? Can no one believe you are dead?

Why did you leave me, John? That is the heart of the matter. Robert showed me how to read the cowlick on the chocolate shells. All the assorted pieces before him, semisweet and milk, in the pleated paper cups. Each had its own dripping crest that told its center. A crown of thorns for coconut, a halo for cherries.

That is what we all need. Our own braille, like phrenology, to tell us the difference between cordials and hard centers.

I am in Indianapolis. Robert is inviting some friends to come and talk about the world, about its future, about you. I will meet them. I will be as close as they come to you.

I am going through my file of letters to a dead man. One of the first things I learned were your last words, reported by Lt. Tung:

我不能走了

Wo pu neng tsou le. I cannot go on. I cannot go on. Yet I fear we cannot live without you.

◆◆

The Greek Letter
in the Bed

The skull over the door is stolen from the biology lab. There are red Christmas tree lights in the eye sockets. The triangle has something to do with champagne. They don't tell me what. The TKE sign stays on all night. Sometimes, the boys from the other houses steal our light, and, sometimes, my boys steal theirs. They hide them in my suite. My suite fills up with Greek letters. I stack them against the wall with the light bulbs still warm. "You boys," I say. In their plywood frames the bulbs are the size of grapefruit and look like a package that Harry and David, the fruit people, would send. My furniture is alphabetized. When a boy comes in to talk with me about how he misses home, he parks himself on the Tau by my dresser.

These chaise longues must be replaced next spring. The weather wrecks them here on the porch. An alumnus lends us furniture his motel can't use. We have the finest furniture on campus, and that helps at rush. But the alumnus causes problems now and then, appearing unexpectedly at house parties and telling anyone who will listen about the parties they had when he was a pledge. The boys say you are a Teke for life, but I know his only reason for being there is to watch out for his couches. He doesn't want anyone to be sick on them.

Of course, I have my own key and even my own entrance around back over the kitchen, but on nights like this one, I like to use the front door to see who is sleeping in the public rooms and the TV lounge. Make sure they're warm enough. Or I stay up with one and talk about the party. I let him make promises to me that he will never drink again. I pick my way through the bodies. Snores and sour smells. These are the unlucky ones. No one to sleep with so they sleep with each other.

The boys at Wabash call themselves gentlemen. If one of them entertains a lady for the evening, he hangs a knotted tie on the knob of his closed door. There are no locks. Late some nights, when I can't sleep, I walk through the house with my Boston. We troop down a whole corridor of doors sporting ties. Ties I've tied for them. It is the only time they are used. The boys come to my suite with the tie in their hands. I make them stand in the mirror, and I reach over their shoulders, putting together a bold Windsor as a man would do it. I never learned the motherly way of facing them. They slide their ties off, knotted, over their heads. Thanks.

I know why they send me away when they have house parties and mixers with sororities from Hanover or Depauw. One night I found my boys and their dates spread out around the house, peering in the basement windows. They ruined my borders, moss roses and impatiens. Inside, a pledge was earning all of his points by making love to a woman on the billiard table. He was being supervised by his big brother—that's part of the rules. Usually, you earn your points by vacuuming the hallways or cleaning the head. Outside, everybody hedged in between me and the windows. All I could see were two bare feet sunk in the corner pockets. The next night, I asked that pledge to sit next to me at my table during dinner. He gave the prayer and nothing else was ever said about it.

They send me away on Thursday nights so they can tell their dirty jokes and have food fights or drop eggs from the third-floor landing, trying to hit the heads of pledges in the basement well below. Or the girls arrive for a football weekend. Most of the boys will be lawyers or doctors, and most of the girls want to be those kinds of wives. Meanwhile, I am with the other house-mothers in a cottage off campus, playing bridge very fast, eating desserts our cooks make, and boasting about our boys. I wish sometimes we would play euchre instead. Loll says it is not seemly for housemothers to play it. She is from Sig Ep and yaks on about her dead husband. "A man," she says, "like no other man." As if she knew. "Loll," she says he said, "you are like no other woman." And he would know because he knew a couple of the other housemothers back when we were all younger. He was the football coach and most of the housemothers are local girls. I don't think Loll knows. That's when Dorcas will say, "Mighty fine Texas cake, Marcella." And Marcella will answer, "Well, thank you, hon. More nuts this time." They are partners and Loll snips at some code. It's code, all right. All of us have lived too long. Too long with boys. Too long without anything else. Room and board are free, remember. And the boys are always the same age. It keeps me young. The campus never changes. Most of the time we are the only women around. And the boys pretend to be gentlemen. I feel as I have always felt.

Here is a story I always want to tell at those card parties. When I went to Washington, I visited the Capitol. In a room that has all these statues, there is a certain spot you can stand on and hear what's being whispered on the other side of the room. Hear every word. My room is like that hall. That is how it is in my room in the house. The heating ducts and tunnels, the thin panel-ing and the laundry chutes must all crisscross above my bed. Nights, I hear the sounds the couples make in the rooms, and I know they are listening, too, to one another through the walls. This is what I want to tell the other housemothers. Listening as if I were on the bottom of some sea with all those noises swim-ming around my bed, I breathe out a kind of moan and listen to the middle of it being picked up and passed from one mouth to another, sinking back into the new wing where there are bunk beds, a couple above and a couple below, and back again. Each room adds its own layer and then it comes to me, a round dollop of sound, suspended above me. And me, the mother of pearl. No, I never interfere. That is not what a housemother is.

Thursday nights in the cottage are for buttermints and the little stadium pillows Blanche brings for the folding chairs embroidered with "Sit on Depauw." Autumn nights, we can hear the boys singing. One house might come by to serenade us, singing "Greensleeves" and "Back Home Again in Indiana." Or a wife of some faculty member will bring a covered dish and her Avon samples. But we don't have much truck with the wives. We aren't wives now, after all. Not mothers either, except to places, to houses. And because we keep houses, we are thought to be deaf and dumb. I probably am. We are for appearances only and our appearance—the same Butterick pattern in sixteen fabrics. "I thought that man would be the death of me," Loll says. "Always after me." Some nights we play hearts instead.

Nor will I tell them about that fellow, Pound, the crazy poet, and how I was the one who made him leave this place. When it is my turn to deal, I deal. But it is true. I was the woman in his room that night. Because of me he went to Europe, and that's where he got famous.

I was with a circus that fall, and Crawfordsville was the last show before we wintered at Peru. I took tickets mostly, guessed weights and ages on the little midway we had. I read minds. I stayed in Crawfordsville after being paid off, hoping to go south. I spent the first night in the open with some flyers who next day left for parts unknown. That's how I met Mr. Pound, near a mailbox on Grand Avenue. He was mailing a stack of letters—there must have been twenty. He was mailing them one at a time, reading each address before pushing each envelope in the slot. He wore a big white Panama, and he had a malacca cane. Not to mention a red beard.

"You look cold," he said.

"I am cold," I said.

I was cold. Crawfordsville has never been friendly to a single woman. The college is all men. The town is used to men. At the circus, most of the crowd was made up of boys from the college in collarless shirts and crew-neck sweaters, hanging around an older man, a professor. What girls there were always carried an armful of dolls and teddy bears, those were just becoming popular, escorted by the boys who kept winning the prizes. I was waiting for a Monon passenger going south.

"You must stay with me," he said. "I need someone to talk to, and you'll do very nicely." He rapped his cane against the mailbox. "Besides, it will be fun getting by the housekeeper."

The day had been bright but never warm with those flat-bottomed, fast-moving clouds that seem to make the land flatter and the wind colder. Now that it was night, it had a head start to the first frost. Besides, it was nothing new. I had been in a circus.

"You must tell me my fortune," he said. I went to his rooming house. The stair was opposite the front door. His room was at the top and to the right. He went first and made the housekeeper make some tea, following her to the kitchen. I snuck in and up the stairs. The room was small—a bed, some chairs. Doilies and fringe. There was a big square pillow with a needle-worked "P" that I thought stood for his name but he said later it was for Pennsylvania, where he had gone to school. "Your girl makes you a pillow there. It's all the rage."

"You have a girl?"

"No," he answered.

The tea tasted good. It was English tea. He had some cold cornbread in his pockets. He gave me the bed and put the chairs face-to-face for himself and lit a cigarette without asking me.

"There is much literary tradition in Crawfordsville, you know. Lew Wallace, the author of *Ben Hur*, died here." He said he visited Indianapolis just to see James Whitcomb Riley, that he'd found him entertaining schoolchildren on his porch, a little girl on his lap. Mr. Riley had suggested they get drunk. And, later, they did.

"Won't she hear us?" I said.

"She thinks I talk to myself."

He must not have been a poet then. He talked about the provinces in France because he had been there the summer before. "Hills and peaks and castles," he said. "Not this flat Athens of the Midwest." He was lonely and young. You could tell that. The boys in the Teke House today would have thought him strange, a sissy. The way he dressed. He never did anything but talk to me. He told me about his friends in Pennsylvania and how he loved to take baths. There was something in his voice. The way he talked was like writing a letter. He stretched out in the chairs, throwing his head back and closing his eyes. He fretted about not being happy here or not wanting to stay in Indiana. "I shouldn't feel that way," he said. "I'm a nomad, you see. You are too, aren't you? Don't you want to stop wandering? Don't you want to stay someplace?"

I didn't. I suppose if I could have known about it then, I would have headed out to Hollywood. Instead, I went to sleep, listening to his voice, wondering why there are so few people with red hair. I never told his fortune. Were there leaves I could read? I was his fortune. Behind the red hair was a blue wall, and the ashtray and the tea tray were filled with cigarette butts.

I woke up the next morning and the first thing I saw was Miss Grundy, her arms full of sheets, looking as if she was disappointed I wasn't dead. "That man," she said. "You poor girl." He was fired that morning by President Mackintosh. I was told Ezra begged to stay. It was understood nothing happened between us and that I was not the reason he was dismissed. The trustees thought it a charitable action, suggested Wabash was not suitable for Mr. Pound. I gave Ezra my ticket, and that night he was on his way south to Indianapolis, pillow under his arm. Miss Grundy suggested the college find me a position. Next thing you know, I was centering a canned cherry in the middle of each chocolate pudding in the TKE house.

I got a letter from him, care of Miss Grundy, a few months later. "Venice, a lovely place to come to from Crawfordsville, Ind."

The other mothers wouldn't care, anyway. We swap recipes, sour cream cookies and butter brickle bars. We plan menus and really worry about color on the plate. The price of tea in China. And the boys don't dream. The ones who know who he was and that he was here, never ask me. I hear his name sometimes after English 3. Another gentlemen with a girl in his room. He forgot his tie. Maybe if I was a poet, I could tell them how it was. Instead, I am quiet at my table. The only thing I'm asked about, besides the salt, is when the letters were stolen and when they were returned. And if it's true that the skull is all that's left of the one pledge that told the house's secrets.

Walking through the halls at night with my Boston, I look at the annual pictures. Mine is the only face that never changes. My vanity. It is the same picture every year since the first year. That peek-a-boo look. I had skull-tight hair, veiled eyes, dark, bow lips. What a funny way to grow older and stay younger. The matting is the same every year—a circle for me, their sweetheart and their favorite. The boxes are filled with boys aging over four years like presidents in office. When I meet the real mothers during parents' weekends, I look for the faces in those faces. The way I stare must make them uncomfortable. "Boys," I say, "will be boys."

I saw that Pound again in 1958 when he was in the hospital. I took my vacation that year in Washington so I could try to see him. Ever since the war, *The Star* had run these articles about him because he had been here once. I didn't think I would be able to see him. I was too early at the hospital, so I waited. At two, another woman arrived. She had the profile of a face on a coin. I found out later it was his wife. She never said a thing to me but hello. She had an accent. I followed her and a man in a white coat up a metal spiral staircase. We went down a hallway. In an alcove by a window, I was introduced. He couldn't remember me, of course. But that's because he was sick.

"Indiana," he said. "Elephants walking in the corn."

He made tea. He talked about Italy. There was a chance then that they would let him go in the care of his wife. She sat with her back to the window. Other patients came up to the screen that divided us from the ward. He gave them pennies and sent them away. He wore a green visor cap like a card player or a banker. I thought of crumbs in my lap, and I brushed my skirt with the side of my hand. He talked about Idaho and maybe going there. The potato.

Other people visited. They called him E. P. He talked about poetry to them. I thought then: Had I been a poem? Maybe I was a poem. The only other visitor I recall was another woman because she was from Fort Wayne. She could remember walking the tow path on the canal. She talked to him in Greek. She told me that later. Then, I was watching two of the other patients dancing. Two men, dancing.

I gave him a pound cake meaning a little joke by it, or a token of who he was.

"It's got a pound of butter, a pound of flour, and a pound of sugar," I told him.

He smiled at that. I knew he didn't remember me.

I followed his wife and the other woman out of the hospital. The woman took me back downtown in her limousine.

"He's an old fart," she said, "but important." She said that Wabash was a good school. "I taught in an all-girls' school in Baltimore for years. I have never been back to Indiana. I must go back sometime before I die." I thought that was a strange thing to say.

I went back to Indiana on a night train. The cars were powder blue, and the trip through Ohio seemed to take forever. Have you been through Ohio? I would like to say that the boys missed me, but my vacation is during initiation in the house. That is in early January. They are too busy to miss me. I would like to say too that I was important to someone, to E. P. maybe, but that would not be true. I'm simply one of the somethings that happened to him. I didn't change myself. Or I'm left over, an extra part. The clock still runs. What happens to yeast in bread? There's no story here. He took the stories with him. I think people think sometimes that they make up their own world. There always has to be people like me in those made-up worlds. Nothing would happen if there weren't.

Did I tell you what I do when the nights are cold like this one? I put a big Greek letter in my bed and plug it in. The lights are so bright, they bleach the blankets. It looks like a person curled up in bed. When I get home, it is nice and toasty. I pull back the covers like I was opening a living thing. I look at the huge θ or π lighting up my bed. And my room's all upside-down because the light's coming from below. What does it look like? It looks like nothing else at all. It looks like a letter in a bed.

You must see it sometime. That skull, it never sleeps. Do you need a place to stay?

✦✦

Schliemann
in Indianapolis

1 April 1869

There are twelve great railroads that cross this city now, and the number will be fifteen, I am told, by the end of the year. Three lines pass behind the house I've taken on Noble Street for the sake of my case. My days and nights are filled with the ringing of bells, the huffing of the engines. I sit at this desk thinking about Catherine and my divorce from her, of Serge, Nadja and Natasha in St. Petersburg where they will live and die on account of their mother's foolishness while all the time I hear the constant slipping of steel wheels on steel rails. There is no greater testimony for the future of this country than this ceaseless traffic. My small back yard is filled with white sand that spills from the tracks as the engineers maneuver their machines up the grade. The neighbors' laundry is always sooty, but the stones of our building are still too new to have turned color.

I have engaged the lawyers, five in all, of two firms: Hendricks, Hord and Hendricks as well as Seidensticker and A. Naltner. I believe Senator Hendricks suggested the other firm as they too are German. We filed suit just in time as the court has since adjourned and will not sit again until 1 June. The principal tenor of my complaint is being, by law, published once a week in a weekly paper of general circulation. The advertisement will run for the next six weeks. So I will sit and wait for the court to sit again, pretend I am a resident of this city, and read my challenge to Catherine in the Indiana State Journal. These are the best circumstances I have found for initiating such a complaint. If I fail here I am prepared to try Wisconsin but that will mean fall in Asia Minor and little time to begin digging before the wind turns around or the Turkish government again changes its mind.

My desire to prove my claims on the Troad had brought me to North America for the fourth time. I believe my American citizenship, recently obtained in the city of New York, will aid in my negotiations for a new *firman* with the Turkish government, for they will have little to do with a German and even less with a Russian. To present myself as a Greek would be unthinkable, though I believe more and more that Hellas is my homeland. I am fortunate to be able to choose my citizenship. My fortune is not bounded nor am I restricted by languages. The divorce is an afterthought, an anecdote, and this formality, this waiting, an inconvenience to be sure but an easy one to suffer to be rid of Catherine with her orthodoxies and her precious St. Petersburg. I have come to America for papers only, and I will have them. Indiana is my die, then, for my future direction is clear to me. I need only strip the mistakes of my past from me so that I am left with the golden thread.

I left New York on Wednesday last by the Jersey Central Railroad, then by the Pennsylvanian. I paid $20.00 to Indianapolis and $3.00 for baggage. For $2.50 more I had use of a splendid sleeping car called the Silver Palace. In this car were eleven silver columns; splendid silver lamps, in fact, everywhere silverplated ornaments in great profusion; immense numbers of mirrors in silverplated frames, excellent toilettes, magnificent carpets, silken curtains, good waterclosets and stoves, excellent sleeping apparatus. I had good company and among the rest a lady of French descent, even born in France, who had married a man of whom she severely complained saying that he is a drunkard, constantly beats and otherwise ill-treats her. She fled from him on Good Friday when she had been attacked again by this man for not having prepared for him some meat which he did not think sinful since he is from England. I lamented her sad fate but that is all I could do for her. Being without means, she is returning to her husband.

Stories such as this agitate me for I believe in marriage. That I dwell on their telling and on my own state follows from my condition here.

Indianapolis lies at latitude 39.55° and longitude 86.5°. I am 527 feet above the sea, 827 miles from New York. Though it is much colder than New York I must find a place to bathe.

6 April 1869

I am bathing in the White River beneath a railroad bridge where the pilings have created a small beach of sand. As the trains pass overhead, wreaths of the engine's smoke descend in one piece through the laced iron struts and wooden ties. It is quite cold in the water but I believe it is doing me good. It is not the sea, as salt water is indeed healthful. It is not even a river, actually, but a shallow stream where even in its middle I can stand and wave at the passing passenger cars. And this is the principal source of water, along with a few deep wells, for the city. I asked Naltner about this. I see now, that an adequate water supply was not even a consideration for the men who founded Indianapolis. The city was built overnight. It is the newest of cities in the state, evolved from nothing save a swamp. There was not even an Indian village on the site. No one had lived here before. It is an example of parthenogenesis and pride. I am taken by this. Here are a people who build cities for no other reason than that the locations are geographical centers of arbitrarily decided governmental regions. Reason enough. There is no water here, and the past is no deeper than the White River lapping at my waist. No, no deeper than this coat of dust on my new desk.

Naltner has shown me the ruins of the dry canals, finished, after years of labor and extravagant expense, only a few weeks before the first railroad entered town. Horses were to tow barges from New York and the Great Lakes to the Wabash and the great rivers beyond. Now they are grassy ditches that fill sometime with rain. All sorts of rubble, building blocks and timber, everywhere. We rode our horses along the bottom of the perfectly straight canal, seeing nothing on either side but the abandoned banks here and there sprouting spring flowers. The lock doors, sprung open, hung on great useless hinges, and the channels stretched out of sight broken only by mounds of discarded property—furniture and stoves, bed ticking and clothing. The system was never used. The company that built it, bankrupt. There was a man who was bathing in the waterfall created by the broken trough of a feeder aquaduct overhead. He told us only to go away and leave him alone. We did and continued to follow the great cuts. Here: pickaxes, shovels, bars, wedges, and other tools. There was equipment for a drag line. We emerged finally far beyond the limits of the city; the trench had prevented us from seeing the mean shacks at the city's edge. We came in to a field of timothy and clover, a farmer's pasture. We turned our mounts back toward Indianapolis, now only dark smudges of smoke in the distance. There was a street sign in the middle of the field, *125th Street,* and stakes in the ground. We followed these signs in descending order, through the fields to town, to the streets that have been constructed.

My lawyers suggested I purchase a partnership in a local starch factory as evidence of permanent residence in this place. The house, I understand, is not enough so I have arranged to buy a fourth of a share of the Union Starch Company on New York Street for $12,000 with $350 of it in cash. The terms are put in such a way that I will forfeit my share if the balance is not forthcoming by 25 July. By that time, if all goes well, I will be in Europe. The sum is not too great to lose.

I am reading the books Doctor Drisler suggested on the Indian languages. They are Gallatin, Buchanan, Catlin and W. W. Turner. Perhaps, as I wait here, I can learn a few of these tongues. But my method depends upon simultaneous reading of a book printed in the new language as well as one printed in one of the languages I know. I have found no book in the languages I know translated into the Indian and no book at all of the original Indian dialect. Is there writing? I am still working on Swedish and Polish, and Naltner reminded me that I can find speakers of all my languages within my neighborhood. Yes, but what would I say to these fellows? No one must know the real purpose for my presence here. I am alone in this small house. I have outfitted it with simple furnishings. I read all day. I write letters and receive answers.

17 April 1869

Last night a hurricane blew up with such sudden force and power I was afraid this house would be knocked down. Accompanying the storm were rain, hail and lightning. I stood by my window and waited for the next illumination of a grotesque frieze: the saplings bowed, stripped of their young leaves; crazed horses with men at their harness; children reaching to grasp their mothers' skirts. Scarcely had the storm begun and the sound of its machinations drowned the puny chuffings of my backyard rail line, when a larger explosion sounded, the shock quaking the ground and seeming to take even the tempest by surprise. Soon thereafter the fire alarm rang out, and I went at once from window to window. I saw no fire from any vantage, but stood transfixed by the lightning and the unnatural tolling of the alarm. I saw again that night in San Francisco, my first trip to America. Having come to join my brother and his mining concern, I found instead I would bury him, dead from typhus, in the hillside he had sought to excavate. I am a broker. I saw an opportunity in trading with the miners while I settled my brother's affairs. I assayed ore, advanced credit, took risk. I awoke that dreadful night to a similar alarm; the windows were filled with flame. I escaped to the bay with one pud of dust on which I sat and watched the hills that city was built on blaze golden against the black sky. My brother's body lay somewhere beneath that storm of fire.

The day after the storm in Indianapolis I learned that the hurricane had collapsed the Central Railroad Freight Depot and buried nine people. Seven escaped, slightly injured, but two, one being the Reverend Daniel Ballou, a Universalist Minister of Utica who had preached at the Masonic Hall, died today. Already the citizens of the city begin to rebuild with workers making hardly an attempt to salvage brick from the previous walls.

Today the weather is again much cooler.

26 April 1869

Today was the anniversary of the foundation of the Odd Fellows society in consequence of which a great festival was held with great processions of the Odd Fellows in their uniforms or grades of distinction in the streets with many banners and much music.

I read again today my notice of divorce from Catherine. I also read her letters, the ones placed in evidence, with their botched translations which make her sound the schoolgirl. Her Russian is far more eloquent, her pleas better constructed, and I hear somewhere within her phrasing the old music. Or is it my recollection of the language itself and the time when I was new to it. I have made love to that woman in my fifth language. My vocabulary is exhausted. "My husband," she calls in her letters "I will always be here," she says. Sometimes it is a curse to know all the different names for a thing. Husband. Wife. One longs for the dead tongues and a world that does not change. I am

the papers printed in languages other than English as well. There is even a paper in Hebrew that is delivered. My cook—herself an avid reader of the press, as Americans believe the press to be the fount of knowledge, the means of advancement while the papers do not attempt to show that it is otherwise—now is convinced I am a Russian Jew. She speaks slowly to me in English when she brings my tea, as if I were a child.

Here, more notices of storms. We have had tremendous rains and in consequence heavy inundations which have nearly destroyed the bath at the bridge. The storms are accompanied by thunder, and the paper is filled with the sad news of persons struck dead or maimed by the flashes of lightning.

The temperature changes all of a sudden.

10 May 1869

No one believes the city exists. Learned men tell me it is all metaphor, a creation of Homer, nothing more. "You are a grocer," they say, "a dealer of dry goods." They are inaccurate when they attempt even to describe the thing before them. They see only what they have been told to see and are polite since they wish to continue their sterile diggings and the search for antiques. They believe in my wealth that it might give them aid as they scratch in a place not one meter deep. They speak of imagination. Surely they can see that the world is very old, that even the fanciest poetry contains a buried truth. The swamp on Mr. Calvert's land in Hassilk can be read. Odysseus tells Eumaeus that hard by the walls of Troy was such a swamp. And beyond the hill the continuous range of more hills.

As a general rule, classic literature is despised here owing to the universal enthusiasms for acquiring material wealth; thus classical education is at low ebb. Knowledge cannot hold out against the same desire. The colleges answer perfectly to the German gymnasiums.

Thus at every turn I am not understood. To some I am nothing but a common man. Here, a savant entombed in books and papers who is not of this world nor takes part in the life of Indianapolis. I dream of Troy. The towers and gates. Of pulling it to the surface whole, brushing it off, and placing it before them. But the Turks will have left buried only the reliefs and statues of gods and beasts as they quarried the stone. The *Koran* forbids the representation of living things. Let me raise these beings then and the dumb stones will fall in place.

13 May 1869

I am taken by the enormous amount of children who seem healthy and very pretty for the most part. The immigrants—German and Irish—seem to produce more than the Americans who are far less blessed with offspring. Many of these scions, I have found, are already engaged in making their own way, earning their bread while boot-blacking, running errands, selling the continuing stream of the newspapers' updated editions. I recall one lad who placed a booklet on the laps of each patron of a horse-drawn omnibus I was riding. The booklet depicted various views of the city, mostly of the capitol. He told us all that they were 3 cents apiece, 2 for 5 cents. I gave him a dollar, and he carefully counted out the exact number, calling me "Sir" and telling me that he wasn't a beggar. He exited as the car stopped and disappeared into a street crowded with children and crisscrossed over head with numberless telegraphic wires.

The vegetation has rapidly advanced.

14 May 1869

My worst fears have been realized as the governor has called the legislature into extraordinary session having to do with appropriations and the passage of the 15th Constitutional Amendment that concerns voting rights. Introduced this session as well was a bill amending the existing divorce law. Its drafting was motivated by the recent sensational divorce scandal, and its passage pricked on by aroused public sentiment. The bill, if passed, would allow a divorce only after a summons had been presented and sworn to the defendant. The plaintiff must be a longstanding resident of the county, attested to. There is also a most urgent clause attached that would affect my case, since, as law, it would become immediately enforceable. A summons would be dispatched to Russia and my wife, causing an intolerable delay.

Since the inauguration of the special session, I have visited the capitol daily. I have been endeavoring to prevent this bill's passage in its present form.

The capitol itself is an amalgamation of classic columns and domes, the central one of hammered gold. The stone is the state limestone. Upon close examination there appears in the grain a solid sea of frozen invertebrates, shells and such, worms and snails, all petrified. Creatures turned to stone. I thought of the marbles on the exploded Parthenon and of finding the toe beneath my feet. I thought of the smoothness of those stones and how they would fit back together. I pointed out the teeming life to Naltner, who was there to introduce me to various legislators. He said he hadn't noticed that before. All stone was field stone to him, and he then showed me the overlarge statuary of Washington, Jefferson, and other founders draped in competently rendered togas, the periwigs chiseled to their heads. "Italians," he said.

I sat in the public gallery of the Senate along with the ladies who vigorously fanned themselves and watched the passage of the divorce bill. I had been too late to prevent it. The ladies were satisfied, applauding politely all around me. In the house the bill was referred to a committee, which would allow time to plead my case before what Naltner assured me was to be a key collection of representatives. The meeting is being arranged for a few days hence. I watched the house in session, standing by the door and its man. I am not hopeful of the outcome. The representatives behave much like schoolboys, all chewing and continually spitting. Many hold their legs up on their desks before them, and all put the laws in the most summary and reckless way.

I left Naltner there departing from him in the darkened rotunda. Again, there were more assurances. Emerging from the shadows of the capitol out into the now darkening streets of Indianapolis, I saw the veterans making their ways back to the grounds. This is where they sleep. One meets them here at every step. Men with only one arm or one leg and sometimes even worse. Both legs amputated. I saw even one whose both legs were amputated close to the abdomen. They come here for the pension accounts and do not return home. Along the streets are men in the dusty dark blue tunics. Yellow piping for the cavalry, red for the artillery. The braid and decorations are peeling from the sleeves. The hats have been stripped of their badges. They talk in groups. They light torches. They pose in the circle at the city's center, prefiguring the statutes the legislature promises to erect at public expense. Everywhere there is this blue and suddenly I realize it is my blue. I was the merchant of this color. It was my indigo warehoused from the Crimea. It was my dye in their coats. The color has bled as well. It is the exact shade of the sky at that time of the evening. The color the sky absorbs when the sun sets over a prairie, over something as broad as the sea. It is no longer Prussian blue or Russian or Austrian. It is an American blue. There are Zouaves too in faded short jackets. The fez crushed. The loose striped pantaloons flap as the man swings by on a crutch. I am reminded of the Turks, my own adversaries, standing on the hillside overlooking the digging. The rifles cross the knees. I look out of the pit as out of my own grave, up at the guards who are smoking and talking. Nightly, I pass these crippled men wearing the memories of what has happened to them. I am aware of the elaborate procedure of my own walking. The soldiers make their way by me like shadows, but they are not shadows.

At home again, I am too despondent to open my letters. I ignore the package from Archbishop Vimbos though I know it contains the portraits I have requested.

16 May 1869

I met the legislators in the adjourned and abandoned Supreme Court room of the capitol. The room is a perfect cube. These dimensions symbolize something I am sure. The walls contain portraits of retired justices. The more recent are daguerreotypes or other photographs. Naltner explained the circumstances of my case. He explained who I am, my books, my ideas about Troy. The legislators on their part look unimpressed, their gazes as glassy as those emanating from the rows of pictures. I assured them of the seriousness of my suit. I spoke of my starch factory in the city, my recent purchase of shares in the Chicago, Burlington, and Quincy and other roads, my desire to stay in the state. Arrangements were made. They were amenable to a deletion of the urgent clause, saying they saw no difference a month or two delay in implementation would make in the spirit of the law. We agreed, as we descended the broad stairs to the floor of their chamber, that the current law was an abomination, that its abuses should be curtailed. And I did agree with them as I shook their hands in an ante-chamber, a room full of men shaking hands. I tire, though, of the pretense. I have created this elaborate life of lies. I do this in order to one day scratch in the dirt. My languages have only helped me lie in every tongue. I lie even to myself. This too is necessary. This is another thing that must be done. I am so positive I am correct. I can see so clearly. The picture of the place, that city, aches in my brain, and all these words in all the languages ever spoken cannot place stone back on stone.

I sat the rest of the day in the gallery as the debate continued below. I listened to speeches made on a variety of subjects—

commodity prices, allocations, penal code, the amendment to the Constitution—while everywhere on the floor knots of men stood in the chamber's corners, at their desks and in the doorways and whispered without gesturing nor listening to what was being said.

17 May 1869

The temperature changes here are very sudden. Some days ago it was cold, and it was necessary to light heaters and put on heavy clothes. In a few days a heat wave caused the temperature to rise to 39° in the shade. On account of the humidity, the heat is unbearable and oppressive. Since the city is surrounded by swamps, the heat causes pestilential infections—ague, Isthmus fever, erysipelas. At least one-third of the population is afflicted with fevers. As a prophylactic measure, every morning I take a little quinine which I trust grants me immunity.

I will leave my daughter, Nadja, this house. It amuses me to think of her here in some far future time, perhaps reading this entry while she sits at this desk. How many railroads will there be then? Will she attempt to piece together the mystery of why her father left her so young and then disappeared into America. I had hoped to teach each of my children a special language, one only each would know. Serge, Italian. Nadja, Finnish and Arabic for Natasha. Instead I will leave them houses all over the world. They will learn their own languages. I see her on the way across the sea, holding her hat as she stands near the railing. I see her reading this page, looking for a mention of her mother's name, her own name. Until then this house will bring an income of $144.00 minus commission to Naltner which is altogether satisfactory.

I have been at the capitol daily. Soon the bill will be read for its third and last time. Pierce's amendment which I supported was tabled due to its length. Another died for a want of a second.

21 May 1869

I am already in love with the photograph. My friend and teacher the Archbishop Vimbos, at my urgings, has sent these portraits. I had written to him in February explaining my future plans and my desire to have a Greek wife once I was free of my Russian one. I told him that I sought a wife of the same angelic character as his married sister. She should be poor but well educated. She must be enthusiastic about Homer and about the rebirth of my beloved Greece. The languages, I told him, do not matter, but she was to be of the Greek type with black hair and if possible beautiful. My main requirement was a good and loving heart.

Her image is here before me, immediately recognizable as the loveliest among tin plates of the others. She is young. Not twenty, I would guess. I fancy myself as living now only in a metaphysical world. I desire a wife who is inclined toward learning, one who would simply love and honor me and travel. I was once sensual and sentimental, but I have changed through those long winters. Perhaps a widow, I suggested. A girl, after all, finds paradise in the fulfillment of her physical desires. But the baths, the baths have invigorated me, and I have refrained from daily horseback riding while in my bachelor's state. The light on the plate turns her face silver, an icon, surrounded by ebony enamel. Her black hair. I am an old traveler and a good reader of faces. The others ring of tin, smell of mercury. In their visages is always something blurred: the eyes both closed and opened; the mouth, a smile and frown; a hand sweeping to brush back the vanishing hair. Not Sophia's face. Her eyes are clear. Her skin is bright. How like noble Paris I feel, choosing among the goddesses. But beyond the myth, the bride is no mere mortal woman. How this little piece of foil draws all the light in this dark room, the yellowing newspapers and heavy curtains. It is the only light in this dark summer. The question is still undecided which will free me to go to her. I cannot read what is before me. I find it impossible to read what I am writing. My eyes, old and weak, are drawn to her face. I wonder, does she play the piano?

24 May 1869

I have been bathing here in the river for more than a month, but it appears that there is no other amateur but me for early bathing.

There are no coffee houses here.

The weather has become very hot and the thermometer ranges between 22° and 25° Reaumur in the shade. The air is damp as it rains every day. One feels the heat double.

I visited the Union Starch Manufactory. I am part owner of the company. It is altogether a fine building being three stories made of red brick with large windows. A stream runs hard by. Everywhere, there is white steam escaping and the smell of the matter. It is a new building, completed after a previous factory was totally destroyed by fire a year ago. We have a capacity of 40,000–50,000 pounds of starch per week. But I was feigning interest. I was far more taken with the girls working, their open faces appearing in the partings of the steam. There was a lightness in my step even though the heat was unbearable and several of us were down to our shirt sleeves.

It occurs to me now how inaccurate these journals will be, not a record of each day at all but whole clumps of time. Some passages were written in passion, others on sleepless nights. How much do I carry with me? And these few facts, will they be important when I leave this place?

If all fails there is Wisconsin which has written its desire for citizens into its divorce laws. It is a part of the country that I have yet to see.

29 May 1869

To my greatest joy 41 of the democratic members presented their resignations to the governor in order to avoid voting on the 15th amendment to the United States Constitution which gives to the former slaves the right of voting. By their resignation the House had no quorum and thus no more business could be transacted. The remaining republicans with but 3 democrats who remained voted then on the 15th Amendment, with but 3 nays, the democrats. It is doubtful it will be sanctioned by the Congress. At all events no other business could be done by the House. No further action will be taken on the divorce bill. My joy is immense. After all, I am very glad to have got an insight into the doings of these people's legislative assemblies, which presents Democracy in all its roughness and nudity with all its party spirit and facility to yield to lateral influences, with all its licentiousness. I often saw them throwing paper balls at each other and even the speaker.

1 June 1869

There are now but a few weeks before the court considers my case again and I have every confidence that the adjudication will be in my favor. I am tempted to travel once again, to see the surrounding countryside or the other principal cities of the state. Naltner warns me that the fruition of these plans might suggest my unwillingness to stay permanently here. I am a resident, a citizen. "Go," he says, "go to the local gatherings. The lectures, clubs, performances." I find the theatres dark and undecorated and do not understand the native love of humbug. Barnum, say, and minstrelsy. I brood in this room. I try not to think of Sophia and my case, but I find I wish for the remaining weeks to be over all at once. I compose list after list of questions which I post to Archbishop Vimbos: *What does her father do? Is she a good housekeeper? Can you send me a lock of her hair?* In care of my address in New York. In care of my home in London. Paris. I wait for the mails and the sound of my housekeeper's knock. "Mail," she says. "Letters." All one word sentences for my benefit. These are the longest days of the year.

The sun remains at the zenith constantly. The nights are long also. They only seem to be, of course. Time.

4 June 1869

I see here in the evening at every step bright sparks in the air which are produced by the lightning bug. It is said to remain here only one month. The light is produced by the phosphoric matter which the insect carries at its back part.

I believe in progress. I witness its manifestation daily in this country and on each of my various visits. The draining of the land. The speed at which San Francisco was rebuilt after the conflagration I saw. On my last visit I traveled the south of the country, the battlefields and sacked cities. All gone now I understand. The land planted to the future, new road right-of-ways surveyed next to the twisted rails. I visited the patent office in Washington and toyed with the models one must submit. The pavement here is, itself, new and much improved being broad, well drained with wide *trottoirs* for those on foot.

Yesterday I witnessed a demonstration of a recent invention, an engine of war. A Dr. Gatling, an inventor of farm implements, operated his gun for the citizens of Indianapolis and for the officers of the ordnance section of the United States Army. He assembled the weapon he calls a labor-saving device for siege on the broad field known as the mall. The gun was smaller than a standard field piece. It had a limber and caisson. The barrel consisted of many barrels which rotated by means of a crank similar to those found on a mill. The whole operation resembled grinding coffee. The gallery of spectators was swelled by the number of veterans of the Grand Army in the remnants of their uniforms. The local Horse, in smart tunics and busby, drilled before us as the gun was readied. The green field was turned to black earth beneath their parade. And then Dr. Gatling made a brief speech, mentioning his use of the latest ball and cap and powder. At the conclusion of the speech, those closest to him drew back, and he was left alone on the field where he proceeded to crank the machine, bending slightly at the waist, sending forth shot after shot in less than a second each, and each barrel reloading itself. This he sustained for several minutes while the ladies held their hands on their ears. At last with the ammunition exhausted and the gun silent, the onlookers broke out in cheers. Dr. Gatling, on his part, took a slight bow and swiveled his gun on its axis through 360°. It was a spectacular exhibition, and its sight has stayed with me. The use of such a weapon can be easily imagined.

Tonight the atmospheric conditions must be favorable for I can hear the sounds of animals, their bells and bleats, carried to me from the bordering fields. As I walked in the city before retiring, I turned the corner into an empty street and heard the clear bawling of a calf that must have been miles away.

7 June 1869

In this room I am surrounded by paper. There is my letter to Dr. Drisler and the Convention of American Philologists. If all goes as expected now I will miss this meeting in Poughkeepsie. Here my treatise on *The Thousand and One Nights,* seeking to disprove the claim of its Chinese origins. Around me, my fortress of newspapers and journals from which I have quarried this pile of articles, cut from the various columns. The epidemy of train accidents, a dreadful one recently on the Erie. Cures. Divorce laws. Tales of reconstruction in the South. Notices of meetings. The slow, ancient news of Europe.

I find I lose myself in reveries of Sophia, of visiting her classroom and perhaps hearing her recite the scene in the *Odyssey* where the girls come to the river to wash and to play. I must stop myself before I fall to the old sin of pride. Are all these things I contrived and planned ordained to come true? It is an old story. I will them into being.

12 June 1869

I have made one final trip with Naltner north from here to a site
outside of a small town where a circle of mounds are located.
On our way, we passed through field after field ripening into
the raw commodities on which my fortune is based. We saw
acreage of wheat, maize, oats, barley, and rye in the varied
greens and browns. We saw fine teams of horses and mules and
the various new equipment for reaping and threshing, all
brightly painted. Hay was being raked and drying. Everywhere
we turned there was good husbandry and honest toil. At the
mounds, we discovered that all but the steepest part of the hill
was in cultivation. We stood on the crown of one of the largest,
looking out at the squares of fields and townships. We shared
the summit with a herd of cattle which find it pleasurable there-
abouts. Here the beasts escape the flies and feel the slight breeze
that stirs. They are patient and, as I regarded them, I understood
Hera's epithet, the cow-eyed one. They watched us while we
spoke. Naltner told me of the boys of the country following
behind the plows, collecting barrels of arrowheads and tools,
parts of pots and bones. Most is dirt though. But everywhere I
looked I saw that intelligence shaped the land. The mounds are
the only rise on a broad, flat plain and so arrayed as to leave no
doubt of their unnatural composition, perfect in their geometry
and symmetry. "Who was here?" I asked Naltner. "No one knows,"
he said. There has been nothing written about them. It seems
even the modern Indians, the ones who had had intercourse
with white men, were at a loss to explain such things. Probably
no precious metal or quarried stone. A burial tumulus, perhaps
a site of an ancient battle.

17 June 1869

The Americans are wonderful wood cutters. They cut three times
more than anybody else. For one laborer cuts daily two fathoms

at 128 cubic feet each. They also excel in bricklaying and it is wonderful to see how a brick mason lays, in one day, 200 bricks into the walls of a building.

23 June 1869

To my greatest joy my divorce has been decreed today by the judge, Solomon Blair. His only objection was that the children were unprovided for, but as I consented to take them at my charge, it was all right. I will obtain copies of the papers, the whole proceedings, and the decree. It is to their credit that the lawmakers view marriage as a business transaction, a contract that can be dissolved. I will hasten to New York and then to Europe, to Greece. Perhaps there is still time for a walk in Asia. Perhaps Sophia will need more weaning from her parents' home, a journey to the islands, the birth places of the gods. And winging before me, a letter to Catherine who today in our house in St. Petersburg knows nothing of how her life has changed. I can see her in the front room, sifting through the letters and calling cards, sighing in her way, reaching out to pull the cord, and then thinking better of it. Her attention is arrested by a bird's song or the sounds the children are making, French with Nurse. I already know her future, have already scratched out the note that will transform her world.

Here is something marvelous. There are innumerable suicides daily committed all over the country, and they are reported in detail by the papers. Truly a mystery for everything I have seen is an argument against that course of action.

And here a notice of a meeting of the railroads to standardize time. As it stands now each small town and city sets its clock at noon when the sun is overhead so that the traveler, dizzy at each disembarkation, sets his watch anew. There are a thousand different times. The line's schedules are useless since it is a different time everywhere on earth. An observatory in Pittsburgh is to send a telegraphic signal sometime soon.

◆▸

The Teakwood Deck
of the U.S.S. *Indiana*

I stabbed a man in Zulu. It had to do with a woman. I remember
it was a pearled penknife I'd got from a garage. I'd used it for
whittling and the letters were wearing off. It broke off in his
thigh and nicked the bone. It must have hurt like hell.

I did the time in Michigan City in the metal shop where I
would brush on flux and other men would solder. Smoke would
be going up all over the room. They made the denim clothes
right there in the prison. The pants were as sharp as the sheet
metal we were folding into dustpans and flour scoops. It was
like I was a paper doll and they'd folded the jacket on me with
the tabs creased over my shoulders. And the stuff never seemed
to soften up but would come back from the laundry shrunk and
rumpled, just as stiff, until the one time when all the starch would
be gone and your clothes were rags and you got some new.

There was a man in there who was building a ship. When I
first saw it, he had just laid down the keel and the hull looked
like a shiny new coffin. This guy was in for life and he kept busy
building a model of a battleship, the U.S.S. *Indiana*. He had
hammered rejected license plates, flattened the numbers out.
He'd fold and hammer. In the corner of the shop he'd pinned

up the plans, a blue ship floated on the white paper. He had models made from balsa, the ribs showing through in parts. He had these molds of parts he would use to cast, jigs and dies. His tools were blades and snips. The needles he used to sew the tiny flags, he made into antennas on the model. The ship was 1/48th the size of the real thing, as big as a canoe. The men who walked the deck had heads the size of peas. He painted each face differently, the ratings on their blue sleeves. He told me stories about each man frozen there on the bridge, here tucking into a turret, here popping out of the hatchway. He showed me letters from the same men. He had written to them sending samples of the paint he had mixed asking the men who had actually scraped and painted the real ship if this was anywhere near. He knew the hour, the minute, of the day his ship was sailing, the moment he was modeling.

But this was years later. At first I saw the hull. I saw the pile of rivets he collected from the temples of old eyeglasses. He collected spools for depth charges, straws for gun barrels, window screen for the radar. He collected scraps from the floor of the shop and stockpiled them near the ship. Toothpicks, thimbles, bars of soap, gum wrappers. Lifesavers that were lifesavers, caps from tubes for valves and knobs, pins for shell casings. Everything was something else.

At first he started building only the ship but knew soon enough he'd finish. So he went back and made each part more detailed, the guns and funnels, then stopped again and made even the parts of parts. The pistons in the engines, light bulbs in the sockets.

Some men do this kind of thing. I whittled but I took a stick down to nothing. I watched the black knots of the branches under the bark grow smaller with each smooth strip until they finally disappeared. Maybe I'd sharpen the stick but that got old. Finally it is the shavings thin like the evening paper at my feet. That was what I was after. Strip things so fine that suddenly there is nothing there but the edge of the knife and the first layer of skin over my knuckle.

One of the anchors of the real battleship is on the lawn of the Memorial Coliseum in Fort Wayne. The anchor is gray and as big as a house. I took my then wife to see it. We looked around that state for the other one. But only found deck guns on lawns of the VFW, a whole battery at the football stadium near the university. In other towns, scrap had been melted and turned into statues of sailors looking up and tiny ships plowing through lead waves. There isn't enough of this junk. Too many towns have empty lawns and parks.

The deck of the model was the only real thing. He said the wood was salvaged from the deck. A guard brought him a plank of it. He let me plane it, strip the varnish and splinter it into boards. A smell still rose from it of pitch, maybe the sea. And I didn't want to stop. I've seen other pieces of the deck since then in junior high schools made into plaques for good citizens. It is beautiful wood. The metal plates engraved with names and dates are bolted on and near the bottom there is another smaller one that says this wood is from the deck of the battleship. It is like a piece of the true cross. The longer I live in this state the more of it I find in every public building. And that is why I came to the capitol in Indianapolis to see the governor's desk. I heard it was made from the teakwood deck of the U.S.S. *Indiana.*

So imagine my surprise when in the rotunda of the building I find the finished model of the ship in a glass case with a little legend about the prisoner in Michigan City. He'd finished it before he died. The porthole windows were cellophane cut from cigarette packs. The signal flags spelled out his name. It was painted that spooky gray, the color between the sea and sky, and on the stern a blue airplane was actually taking off and had already climbed above the gleaming deck where a few seaman waved.

I felt sad for that con. He spent his life building this. He never got it right. It wasn't big enough or something.

I walked right into the governor's office. I'm a taxpayer. And the lady told me he wasn't there, and I told her I was more interested in the desk. So she let me in. "It's beautiful, isn't it?" she said opening the curtains for the light that skidded across the top cut to the shape of the state. One edge was pretty straight and the other, where the river ran, looked as if that end had melted like a piece of butter into toast. I ran my hand along the length of it, felt how smooth it was—the grain runs north and south—when the governor walked in with his state trooper.

"It's something," he said. He's a Republican. The trooper followed and stood behind him. "It has its own light."

The trooper wore a sea blue uniform with sky blue patches at the shoulders and the cuff. Belts hung all over him. Stripes and creases ran down his legs. Braids and chains. The pants were wool. He watched me. And I looked at him.

Jesus, you've got to love a man in uniform.

I stepped up to the desk and saw my face and the shadow of my body deep inside the swirling wood. I took my finger and pointed to the spot not far from Zulu where I knifed a man and said, "Right there." I pushed hard with my nail. "That's where I was born."

◆▸

Biograph

Iced air. How do they do it? We could've gone to the Marbro, but they don't have it there. I like the sign outside here, snow on top of all the letters. Everybody sitting outside on the street, looking over at the glowing white in the light. Light bouncing off the awnings. People dying in the heat. But you got a little money, and you are in where it's cool. They must take the heat right out of the air. But how do they know which is the hot part? In the loft, one time, placing bets, I saw the guy who runs the machine out in the middle of the street looking at something he held in his hand. The drays and the trucks working their way around him. Only the trolleys creeping up to him, the motorman yanking on the bell. I couldn't hear it because the windows were closed. The iced air. Everybody squinting at the man in the street holding his hand up staring at it, at something in it. Things moving slow in the heat. Boy, it's swell. I want to stay for the whole show. Let my shirt dry out, roll my socks back up.

Everybody's sitting in the dark. Up there in the ceiling they got the little lights that are supposed to be stars. Palm trees in pots up there on the sides of the stage. Ushers in monkey suits by the fire doors. It's like in Mooresville at the Friends with everybody sitting and waiting for somebody to get up and talk.

I could stand up here and tell them a story. Mrs. Mint is the only one who knows, and she's worried about getting back to Romania, thanks to the house she ran in Gary.

She treats me square. No trouble when I stay with Patty. And Patty, still married to the cop, doesn't have a clue.

Thanks me every time she smiles because I'm the one who got her teeth fixed for her.

Smiling at me in the dark.

Jimmie, she says, *when you going to take off those sunglasses. You can't see the movie.* She likes a man who carries a gun, but she can't say why.

The girls down where Patty works all tell her I look like him. I just laugh, buy her a diamond, tell her I work for the Board of Trade.

There's a guy named Ralph Alsman's arrested all the time because he looks like him. The story's in the papers. How he keeps robbing banks.

There's nothing better to do. Rob a bank, go to a movie, buy a paper. It's all the same.

I read the paper all the time, and I start out thinking I don't know the man. Then I think that could be me.

You have to keep your mind busy or you go nuts. Think of Homer beating it by tying string to flies he caught while he stood time on the mats in Pendleton. You go nuts without something to do. You buy a little time out of the heat.

I bet the girls wouldn't know what to do if I was him. Wouldn't want me to really be him. It only gives them something to talk about without no customers while Patty's putting on her hat and I'm leaning in the doorway waiting for her to blow.

I like Patty good enough, with her smile and all. She is nice and heavy leaning on my arm when we walk on the street. My hand will be in my pocket on the gun, and I'll tap her leg with it through the clothes. She'll smile. Our secret. *My husband, she says, only has the revolver they gave him.*

I like Patty. She'll do for now. But she's not Terry.

Sometimes, I think I see Terry in the Loop when I'm down there with a bag of corn feeding pigeons. Out of the house pretending I'm working. I'll be looking at the birds and her legs will walk by and I'll follow them up and something will go wrong.

I want to ask the doll where she got those legs from, but they just clip along through the crowd of strutting pigeons.

It's like that with a day to kill downtown. Her hand waving for a cab. And in the store windows, I see all the things I could buy that she would like. And all the other women, their hair thrown off their forehead just like hers, tilting their heads and thinking that the stuff they see will make them look like Terry. I can't go and get her. South Bend wasn't enough, and they've hidden her in some county jail. For harboring.

There has been a fire on a boat that had a party going on it. A little boy in a sailor hat is crying behind a glass window. It's beginning to fill with smoke in there, and you can't hear him cry. People are jumping off the ship. The railings are giving out, and people are falling into the water. There is a priest swimming with the boys. And then it is night, and the moon is shining, and the burning ship is shining on the water. Along the shore bodies are washing up, and people and police are looking through them.

So, you're out, Pete is saying as we drive south out of Lima. *They'll go up to the farm while we'll go down to Cincinnati.*

You're out, I say. I hadn't seen them since I got parole. I was in Lima by the time they broke Michigan City. Dumb. *I see you got my message,* I say.

in with you two and share a place? He says, *Sure,* without asking the girls. At the Clarendon, we carried the bags with the guns while the boy took the rest. Margaret set out right away to bake the new money. Crumbling the bills as we made fists, then smoothing them out. All the time we talked about what to do next. Not thinking about it at all. It takes time for new money to get old. But it all fell apart when Terry didn't do her bit. She sat and made up for hours though we weren't going anywhere. One day there was no breakfast on the table. What gives?

There's your girl friend, says Margaret.

Terry starts right up. *I can't cook.*

Well, you better start learning, I say.

Pete making a fist all the time and the green squeezing out through the fingers.

If they don't know me, they don't know how to say my name. The *g* is like in girl or gun. When they showed up from the *Star* and *News* at the farm and asked Dad what he thought about me and said the name, Dad just said, *I don't know him,* never heard of me. *But he's a junior,* they said.

That's not my name, Dad said. And he pronounced it for them.

That's all changed now, they said to him.

The old man just sat there right in front of them.

That's okay. Left all that behind. Even left that *g* behind.

Who told me that? Toms of the *Star* in Tucson while we waited for Indiana, Ohio, and Wisconsin to double-cross us. He came up to the bars during the sideshow, all those locals going by to look at us for a quarter. Pete steaming at Leach. Mac saying how great the weather was down there. Toms called me by my real name and told me the story. He asks me if that's how I wanted to be known, by the other name and all. Hell, it wouldn't do any good. It's out of our hands, just like everything else.

The police are leaving after doing nothing. They open the door, and there is a woman standing on the other side just about to knock. Shows she's surprised to see them, but she knows them all by name. She asks them if it is that time of month again. They nod and file out, the plainclothes first and then the uniforms. She stops one who is eating a sandwich as he goes by, takes out a hanky, and polishes his badge. All I had was a big bolt wrapped up in a neckerchief. I kept hitting him but only knocking off his straw hat. He'd pick it up and put it on again, and I'd knock it off. He was making that godawful sound, and I could hear the Masons come running. He didn't have no money. I didn't know a thing then. Just a kid. Same grocer gave me a talking to when I'd swiped some jawbreakers. He knew my dad. I ran, and someone chucked a bottle after me. They found me in the barn.

It was to have been all set. But the judge didn't care. I heard he died falling asleep across some railroad tracks, a knife in his pocket because I was coming to get him.

Since the operation, it's been like I had on thimbles. Patty wonders what's happened to my fingers. She's got them spread out in front of her eyes, tired of my fortune. She says, *Well, hell. How do you pick up something like a dime?*

I start thinking about all the things I've touched. Chairs and guns and the counter I hopped over in Daleville. The glasses. The sinks. The steering wheels. The money. It's like those things remember how I felt. But me, I forgot it as soon as I let go.

Touched Terry all over. Must have left a print on her everywhere. Some cop dusting her rear, blowing it off, saying, *We got the son of a bitch.* And they're all looking at her, looking for me. All the other women too. Shaking hands with men and having them look into their palms.

You think twice about punching a light switch.

Red rushing in saying that he killed a cop at the garage. Lost the Auburn, and they got his girl. He quieted down, started in telling us all over again what had happened and that the girl could be trusted. We looked at each other's faces, knowing that we didn't look like anybody else no more. Mac looked like a banker. Pete like some college kid, he's going without a hat and wearing that floppy collar. He walked into Racine and put a big Red Cross poster on the window without anybody taking a second look. And I'm looking like a sissy bookkeeper. Putting on weight.

We got the girls to dye our hair. Thought it was funny, us sitting with sheets around our necks. I said red and let my mustache grow. Terry sitting on my lap, drawing the eyebrows in. *Didn't like your face to begin with,* she's saying. Pete telling me later about the two toes he's got grown together. And Red holding up his hand, saying, *What am I going to do with these.* I never thought about them before, the fingers he left on the railroad track in the Soo.

They're going to fry you, boy.

I could hear Pete calling from the next cell. Leach was taking me back to Indiana. I fought them off awhile and they put cuffs on too hard for it. Some vacation. There was the cop from East Chicago who ran away. *He tried to stop me,* I tell them. Where is Wisconsin's Lightning Justice now? I could hear Pete screaming from his cell about going to Wisconsin and staying together and Mac calling from someplace else, *See you, John!*

I'll never see them again. I can't remember their faces. They went from Tucson to Ohio when Indiana waived the bust-out from Michigan City. They'll get it for getting me out of Lima.

The last thing is voices.

So long, John. Sioux Falls, Mason City. South Bend wasn't enough. I met their Mouth on the fair grounds to pass them the money. The parachutes dropping from the tower. *Tell them I'll get more.*

Indiana flew me to Crown Point. The pilot said that over there is Mexico.

Blackie has won the boat on a bet. They sit together on the deck with the lights of the city behind them. He asks her what she wants to name the boat. She talks about having a house and family.

It's old-fashioned, *she says but that is what she wants. Then Blackie kisses her, and she stops talking about leaving the city, sailing away.*

We called her Mack Truck. She made breakfast Christmas morning. The fight I had with Terry was all left over from that race driver. I told her to go back to the reservation. *Take my car.* She's packing and crying.

Pete's girl said, *A girl's got a right to choose who she wants to be with.*

But it was like I didn't know Terry no more, and she stopped being pretty.

Christmas in Florida.

Even the joint had snow.

I told her to go where it was snowing, with the race driver. And she left after Red told her how to work the spark on the Ford. *I can buy another car!* I shouted at her.

It was so hot. I sat around in pieces of suits, and the girls giggled about thinking the tide was a flood. They had never seen an ocean in Indiana.

It got hotter the week after Christmas. The papers said we were still raising hell in Chicago. They blame everything on us. On New Year's Eve, people were shooting off firecrackerrs to see the light on the water. Pete's girl got out a tommy gun, and it rode right up when she shot it. I took it from her and fired it out over the waves, a long rip. But it wasn't any good firing at nothing. The tracers just looked so pitiful. Everybody else had girls and was heading for Tucson. I said I was going north and look for Terry. Red said he'd come along. We'd fence some bonds in Chicago.

If I make it to Mexico, I'll never see any of them again. Terry lost in the jails, Pete and Mac in Ohio. We can't pull off the magic trick again. We broke out of too many places. Even if I could walk in with this new face, there'd be no way to walk them out. The farmers they got to sit with them are taking shots at airplanes flying by. South Bend wasn't enough.

I'll never see Sally Rand at the Fair again. Have the woman I'm with tugging at my sleeve to get the hell out of there. But only half pulling, looking up at the stage too, at the feathers and the shiny pieces of paper. A thing like that. You can't stop watching the fans and balloons—because they are moving and changing and her face is floating, floating above whatever it is she's using to cover herself where she has to. The cops making such a big deal of it, standing off to the side, looking just like the rest of us looking up at the parts of her. Hiding like that. She didn't have to hide!

The alarm is ringing on the building. Red is jumpy, getting the money when a cop walks in. He thinks it's some kind of mistake. His blue overcoat is buttoned over his gun. *Just what I was looking for,* but it's trouble. There are more outside. They're lining up behind cars. *Grab somebody and go!* I yell to Red.

Someone says, *Can I get my coat?*

Out the door with the cop ahead of me and someone is calling the cop's name and the cop is running off down the street. I feel the bullet hit the vest. I knocks me back. I shoot at where the smoke is, and get hit twice more. I hear glass crashing and the alarm. I shoot some more at the smoke, see Red go down to the right, grab him, grab the money. My back is to the guns.

We get away in the car.

East Chicago still has Christmas stuff up.

Red took the bullet under his arm. My chest hurts. Red says from the back seat that being shot ain't nothing like being shot.

The ramps are crowded with people. He runs into Jim, and they shake hands, leaning forward and grabbing each other's arms with their other hands. Jim tells Blackie that he is running for DA *and that Blackie's crowd better watch out. Blackie tells Jim that he's all for him and that Blackie's going straight. There is a roar from the crowd and Blackie says,* Dempsey. *They talk about the fight and say that they will have to get together. There is another roar, and Blackie says,* Firpo.

*   *   *   *

Patty wants to hold hands in the dark. Puts my hand on her knee. She's got no stockings on. It's warm between her legs. We're both looking straight ahead. Watching the movie. I'm slumped down and my hat's on my lap. I'd say the man next to me is crowding me. His arm takes up the arm rest.

Her dress is nice. I think about what it's made of, stitch by stitch. What if the parts fell apart? In the shop I made double task, triple sometimes—yoking sleeves, setting collars with a Tomcat. The white thread in the blue work shirts. Thinking of pulling one thread and having the whole thing fall apart. It just feels good now, the cloth and what's underneath. She is moving.

The new DA is tired. Election night and all that. A woman breaks through the crowd and hops into the limousine after him. She says that Blackie sent her. They settle back in the seat and pull a blanket over their legs.

In Tucson, they took us one at a time, and me and Terry just getting back from looking for Indians. She stood there with her fingers crossed and her hands on top of her head. They cuffed me.

I do some shouting. *Hey, I tell you, I'm Sullivan! You got the wrong man!*

Some vacation, says Terry.

They had the prints on Pete and Mac by the time I made it to the station.

I don't know them. That's what I say. The place is lousy with reporters. The cops take me into a room where they start going through papers. They snatch my hand, turn over my wrist.

Well, what do we have here?

One bent down and undid a shoe.

The other foot, Charlie, says a guy.

They look at my heel a long time. I remember Pendleton and the foundry and pouring metal on it to get out of the heat. And then Charlie, he takes my face in his hands, and I say, *Hey.* He holds my head still while his thumbs feel through my mustache, pressing my lip on my teeth, my head down. *This is the guy,* he says.

They open the door and the reporters come in.

Guess who we got, they say.

Where's Indiana? I ask a farmer who's standing in his field. He points to the road crossing just ahead. Terry says, *You can't tell them apart. Illinois looks just the same. It'd be something if they were the colors on the map.*

I stop to change the plates and put the chains on. The roads are thawing and it'll just get worse as it gets warm. My dad won't know me now with these new clothes and hat. I want him to see Terry and the car. Hubert'll be there and the sisters. We'll hide in the barn if anybody comes. The hay will all be gone, and we can shoot baskets in the loft.

It wasn't warm enough for a picnic. But they filled the house with everyone bringing a covered dish and their own service.

I told them all about Crown Point. Once in the front room. Once in the kitchen. The kids on the porch. The men around back. Hubert took my picture with Terry. Then with me alone with the gun. Says he'll not have it developed till they catch me.

The people on the floor kicked the gas candle back and forth. Homer went in to get Red out of the vault. I'd been shot already. Green bent over where the gas shell hit him. We're all crying. I'm holding a girl when we go through the revolving door. It's my right shoulder so it's her I push against the glass.

She gives a little grunt.

Homer's behind me.

We've got people lined up all over. It's like a picket fence.

Red comes out and gets hit. It's coming from up above us and behind. We all get our guns going. The people got their hands up. Lester sets them out on the Buick. Two on the fenders like deer. They're on the back bumper, the running board, between us in the car. There must be twenty.

Slow! I yell.

Homer's reading off the directions when someone on the running board says, *Here, right here is where I live.* We stop and she gets off. Cars go by honking, thinking it's a shivaree. My arm hurts, all crowded in like that. Lester's leaning out the back with a rifle. We stop to let some more off, and he gets out to spread some tacks. I'm thinking that he's getting them under our car.

Some law you got! he's yelling at the locals.

The new DA and Blackie's girl are sitting at a table in a nightclub. A woman is on the stage, singing. After the song, everyone pounds on the tables with little wooden hammers. Then we see Blackie asleep in a room. He wakes up, and magazines fall to the floor. The phone rings, and he answers it. A woman, in bed, is on the other end of the line. She asks him to guess who she saw that night at the nightclub. Blackie hangs up and looks at the magazines.

Tellers always telling you to use the next window. Not believing you unless you have a mask. Walking in the door and wasting a whole clip above their heads. Less chance of shooting maybe, but you never know when somebody will get a wise idea, think they're in a movie.

That boy in South Bend, looking at his hand where the bullet went through.

The sheriff in Lima saying, *I'm going to have to leave you, Mother.*

The bullet that killed him on the floor next to him.

Margaret so surprised when the gun went off on the beach in Florida.

All the things we didn't do too. And did.

They'd draw my face all wrong. I don't smoke. Finding out later, after Pete and Mac got shipped to Ohio, that Leach told the papers to give me all the play.

Didn't matter to Pete.

Blackie closes the door, leaving the body inside. He catches up with his bodyguard, who is waiting by the elevator. It is New Year's Eve. The bodyguard is wearing a derby.

Cops are at the door, Terry says. And I'm a Lawrence something, something Lawrence. *Get dressed,* I tell her, fitting in a drum.

I am always waking up to these things. I can't remember my name. I'd been leaving every morning, heading downtown to make it look like I had a job.

Terry's put her blouse on backwards. She's remembering what happened at Dr. Eye's.

Shots from the hall.

That'll be Homer coming over for breakfast.

Hurry up, I tell her, and spray the door.

Think about the cake the neighbor lady from across the hall brought over the first day, her husband with the pipe, saying he has a crystal set.

Down the back stairs, back out the back door.

Terry dents a fender backing out the car. I'm waiting, watching the door. The birds are noisy in the vines on the side of the building.

The DA is in his office trying on an overcoat. He tugs on the lapels. He bends forward, clutching the coat together to see where it falls on his legs. He checks to see if there is a label. He turns around in it and asks his assistant for his comments. He looks over his shoulder and down the back of a sleeve. It could be yours, *says the assistant.* Yes, *says the DA, standing there, thinking. He's in the middle of the room, bundled up. They bring him another coat, and the DA tries it on. The DA reaches into the pocket and finds a small wooden hammer.*

I heard they let her finish her drink. Then they took her out of the bar.

She'll be out before you know it, Homer was saying.

We were on the Lincoln Highway, heading to his folks. All the

little towns had banks to rob. *They're taking away parts of me,*
I'm saying to Homer, who's humming. We'd been stumbling
through jobs. Losing guns and money. Not even planning anything anymore. Just going in shooting. Trusting the vests.

I'm lost, I say.

*Men are pushing carts of big steamer trunks through the
crowd. A band is playing somewhere. There's a ship whistle blowing. The DA looks at his watch and out over the people. Everyone
is waving and shouting. There is a siren and the crowd gives
way. An ambulance pulls up to the dock. Blackie gets out.*

The shooting started when three guys left the bar to head
home. The cops must have thought they were us. Lester opened
up right away.

He sleeps with that gun.

I took off up the stairs with Homer and Red. We fired some
out the windows, then covered each other to get out the back,
down the bank to the lake. Walking on the far side, we could
hear the shots over the water. Flashes every now and then.

They kept shooting at the house.

We tied up Red's head and caught our breath. Nobody even
knew we were gone. They'd upped the reward that week.

The lake was very smooth, and we could see because of the
moon and stars. They had all different sizes of guns shooting at
the lodge.

*The DA is running for governor. Blackie is at the racetrack.
He looks through binoculars. He sees her in another part of the
grandstand. He goes over and sits down. She says she's worried
about Jim's chances to become governor. Someone is trying to
ruin him, and he won't do anything about it. Blackie tells her
not to worry, that he'll take care of it. He looks at her, tilts his
head, says she mustn't tell Jim they talked.*

Crossing the Mississippi on the spiral bridge below St. Paul.
Pretty tricky since we're coming from the north. We pick up a
tail. They start shooting. I knock out some glass and shoot back.

Homer guns it. Red gets it. Never lucky, Red. His head already tied up from the night before at the lodge.

We shake them on a farm road and leave the car. I hold on to Red in the ditch while Homer goes to flag down a Ford. A family out for a drive, it looks like. Homer goes in the back with them. Red says he needs something to drink. The car could use gas. I stop at a place. The bottles are cold. My hands leave marks on the glass.

A lady opens the bottles for me. I go back to the car and give one to Red and try to give one to the kid in the back.

He's had his lunch already. I don't want him to have it, says the mother.

Down on one lip of the gravel pit, a locomotive is pushing some empty cars around. Piles of snow left over from the winter. It's been easy to dig in the loose gravel and sand. They're pumping water down below. Homer slides the body down through the bushes, and we put him in the hole. We're taking off all the clothes.

You weren't there, I say to Homer, pointing out the scar under Red's arm.

It's how he missed Tucson.

I tie up his clothes. Homer has the lye, but I want to do it. Feel kind of bad pouring it on his face. Turn his hands over and pour it on his fingers.

It smells real bad.

A hockey game is going on. Lots of people hollering. But there's a man in a men's room, two men. You can see them both in the mirrors. One of them says, You wanted to see me? *The other man pulls some paper towels from the rack. He turns to answer the question. It's Blackie. He has a gun wrapped up in the paper towels. When he shoots, you see the flashes coming from the towels.*

They told me later I swallowed my tongue. Last thing I can remember is the towel on my face. *Hotel Drake* in gold. And the smell of the ether.

I should've had a local. But I couldn't stand the thought of that, of looking at them when they did it. I wanted to wake up different.

I was always waking up the same.

The dimple was gone. But I could see where it had been. And the mole left a mark.

I was puffy and sore.

I saw a picture in a newspaper of a boy that turned out to be a picture of all the boys in a high-school class, one face on top of another. It didn't look like anything, and it had all the parts. I remembered that picture, looking at my face. Rob another bank and I'd have to get rid of this one too.

I wonder what I looked like with my face all blue. No way to forget it. That's me, all right.

Homer was thinking twice, cursing the tattoo. Finally went ahead and called it a goddamn mess. Lester sitting around drinking from a bottle of beer changes his mind a couple of times. Keeps what he has. Damn doctor was probably glad to let him.

Blackie sits and sketches all through his trial. The DA is examining a witness. Blackie's lawyer starts to get up to make an objection. Blackie stops him, says, Relax, you've been beaten by the best, *smiles at the DA, who is telling the jury that people like Blackie must be stopped.*

The cops are happy to show us the guns and vests. We act dumb. *What do you call this?* we are saying.

Oh, that. That's your submachine gun.

They have some .45s too.

We tell them we're from the East, doing a story on the crime wave. *Sports is my regular beat,* says Homer.

Yeah, well I've never been east, says one cop.

You should see the Fair in Chicago while you're in this neck of the woods, says the other one.

They talk it up. We listen.

I like hearing about myself. It's like being at your own funeral.

Being tourists got us in trouble in Tucson. Pete telling a cop he thought he was being followed, and the cop saying no. Tourists from the North. And I take pictures of cops directing traffic.

You look good in a uniform, I tell them. The Sam Browne belts. The buttons picking up the light, turning white in the picture.

Pete used to say, *I wish you'd stop that. It's not smart.*

I'd say, *It's my hobby.*

We tell the cops in Warsaw we'll send them the story when we get done writing it.

The governor is in his car, racing to Sing Sing so he can see Blackie before he goes to the chair at midnight. Sirens getting closer, governor's car, motorcycles, everything speeding.

Guess who, I say to Margaret through her door. When she opens it, she knows me right away.

What happened to your face? You in an accident? I try to laugh. It's not her fault. I go on in. She's tough, but she misses Pete. I give her some money from Mason City and tell her about the tear gas and the bag of pennies. She says she doesn't think it would do any good. *You never know,* I say.

I've been down seeing my folks on the farm, I say.

She says that she reads about me all the time in the papers.

You know half of it ain't true.

It wasn't no good with nothing to plan.

She says she was at a dance when I broke out of Crown Point. She says she made sure a cop saw her that night. Says she makes sure a cop sees her every night. She tells me she's thinking about going into vaudeville. People had been around to ask.

I could hear her sister in the next room taking a bath.

It didn't matter now that we had shields. They kept shooting, and the people with their hands up got hit first. The bags were too light. I was working the inside with two guys I didn't know. They were the only ones who would work with us now. Homer was outside with a rifle and Lester by the Hudson.

We walked out and everyone started to get hit. Homer in the head from a shotgun that took the pants leg off a local. I pulled him into the car.

He said we should wear something different when we did South Bend.

New faces. Sure.

So we had on overalls over the vests. Always a clown. We wore straws too. Changed his luck. Pieces of straw mixed in with his hair in the hole in his head. Lester wanted to count the money again.

Blackie walks with the priest. The warden is there, the governor, two guards. Blackie says so long. Someone is playing a harmonica.

Mrs. Mint saying again over ice cream that Romania isn't a country, just what was left of a place after the war. Patty holds the cherry up for me.

I don't know anything about the world.

I'm seen everywhere.

Cops in England are searching the boats going to France. Everybody that turns up is what's left of me.

I could call the Leach home, hear him stutter while he tries to keep me on the line. But it could be anybody with a gun. I'm worth too much now that the governors got together.

I'll check in with Henry Ford. Send a messenger to Detroit with a note. All the models I left on the edge of Chicago. Good little cars.

Mrs. Mint told me she's already turned the bed down back at Patty's place. But I want to stay and watch the cartoons.

The lights are going up and everybody's squinting coming out of the dark. I can see who's been next to me. And Patty crying. Mrs. Mint looking through her purse for a hanky for her. I can't keep my eyes open. Pete, Mac. I'll see their Mouth at Wrigley tomorrow, give him what I can spare from the trip.

Patty touching my hand. Then both of the women are squeezing by, heading for the aisle. The crowd is buzzing and I can smell the smoke from the lobby. It's cold in here. Just this once I'd like to open my eyes and have it be all different.

◆▸

Fidel

My husband, I'll call him David, left me for my best friend. I'll call her Linda. Since then, I have found it difficult to sleep.

I have taken to listening to the radio through the night. The radio is next to the bed, an old floor model filled with tubes that heat up and glow through the joints in the wood frame. My father gave it to me when I left home to live with my husband, I'm calling David. I used it then only as an end table next to the bed. I painted it a gloss red and covered it with house and garden magazines, the bottom one's back cover still sticks to the tacky enamel surface. I live in a city I'll call Fort Wayne.

I listen to a local station, I'll call WOWO. It is the oldest station in town. It's been on the air since the beginning of radio. My father listened to the same station ever since he bought the radio console on time. I have seen the payment schedule. He kept it in the drawer beneath the sad face of the staring dials and the frowning window scaled with AM numbers. He penciled in 37¢ each week after he walked downtown to a store I'll call The Grand Leader to turn over the installment.

One night, when I couldn't sleep, I rolled over in bed and noticed for the first time since I had painted the radio red the two clunky knobs the size and shape of cherry cordials, one to tune and the other the power switch that also controls the volume. Without touching the tuning knob, I turned the radio on, but nothing happened. Nothing happened even after I waited the amount of time I thought it would need to warm up. I turned on the brass table lamp perched atop the pile of wrinkled magazines. I had never plugged in the old radio. I rolled out of bed and onto the floor. Behind the radio was an outlet where the table lamp and the modern clock radio were connected. I had the other radio's plug in hand as I pulled out what I thought would be the plug for the clock radio. It was the plug for the lamp instead. In the dark, I scraped the walls of the bedroom with the prongs of the radio's plug looking for the outlet never thinking to reinsert the plug of the lamp. I had painted the walls a linen white about the same time I had painted the radio red. When I found the outlet the radio lit up inside, green light leaking out every seam and joint. I was sitting on the floor when WOWO faded in, the station my father listened to years ago when he listened to this radio before I was even born.

The next few weeks I listened through the nights and into the morning. I left the radio on during the day for the cats, who I'll call Amber, Silky, and Scooter, as I stumbled off to work each day. They liked the purring box. In the evenings when I staggered back in I'd find them attached like furry limpets to the shiny skin of the radio. The paint, constantly baked by the glowing tubes, gave off the stink of drying paint again and steeped the bedroom in that hopeful new smell it had when I first moved here with the man I am calling David.

The later it got at night the further back in time WOWO seemed to go with the music it played. After midnight scratchy recordings of Big Bands were introduced by Listo Fisher, who pretended the broadcast still came from the ballrooms of the Hotel Indiana. Alfonse Bott, Tyrone Denig and the Draft Sisters, the bothers Melvin and Merv LeClair and their orchestras, Smoke Sessions and his Round Sound, the crooner Dick Jergens who sang with Bernard "Fudge" Royal and his band or with Whitney

Pratt's Whirlwinds, and Bliss James singing the old standards. It was as if I had tuned into my father's era, the music slow, unamplified, and breathy. Toward morning the sound was like a syrup with wind instruments scored in octave steps, the brass all muted, the snares sanded, and the bass dripping.

Bob Sievers, who had been the morning farm show host at WOWO for as long as I could remember, came on at five. I had first seen him, though I had heard him for a long time before that, when I was in high school. On television, he was selling prepaid funerals to old people. He didn't look like his voice. And now I heard that voice again thanking Listo Fisher for standing watch at night and then cuing the Red Birds, a local quartet, to sing "Little Red Barn" as he dialed the first of ten Highway Patrol barracks to ask what the night had been like in the state I am calling Indiana.

The sputtering ring of the telephones on the radio sounded swaddled in cotton. It was five in the morning. My head melted into the flannel of the pillow slip. The only sound was the mumble of the connection as a desk sergeant answered in a place called Evansville. He whispered a sleepy monaural hello encased in the heavy Bakelite of an ancient telephone. Bob Sievers, his bass voice lowered a register, identified himself and asked about the weather down there in the southern part of the state. The flat accents of the trooper reported snow had fallen overnight but that the major roads were salted and plowed.

I waited for the next question, lifting my head from the pillow. Bob Sievers's voice dove even lower, "And, Sergeant, were there any fatals overnight?" For a second I listened to the snow of static, the voltage of the phone picked up by the sensitive studio microphones. "No, Bob," the trooper answered, "a quiet night." Instantly I would hear the ratchet of the next number being dialed, the drowsy cop, the weather outside Vincennes, then South Bend, Terre Haute, Jasper, then on the toll road in Gary, Indianapolis, Mount Vernon, Monon, and finally Peru. At each post, the search for casualties, the crumbs of accidents. Every now and then someone would have died in a crash. The trooper sketched in the details. The road, its conditions, the stationary objects, the vehicles involved, and the units dispatched, withholding the identities of the deceased until the notification of the next of kin.

There were nights I waited for such notification. I saw my husband behind the wheel of my best friend's car, his face stained by the dash light of the radio. He is listening to WOWO, the Big Bands of the early morning, when the car begins to pirouette on the parquet of black ice. I know that the radio is still playing, a miracle, after the car buries itself in a ditch of clattering cattails sprouting from the crusted snow. The last thing he hears, the car battery dying, is the quick muffled dialing of Bob Sievers, his morning round of calls, and the hoarse, routine replies. I think to myself I am still some kind of kin. Those nights, I practiced my responses to the news brought to me by men in blue wool serge huddled on my stoop.

WOWO is a clear channel station, 50,000 watts. At sunset smaller stations on nearby interfering frequencies stop broadcasting and the signal can be picked up as far south as Florida and out west to the Rockies. Just north the iron in the soil damps the power, soaking up the magnetic waves before they spread into Canada. Listening, I felt connected to the truck drivers in Texas and the night auditors on the Outer Banks who called into Listo Fisher and told him they were listening. Often they would ask, "Where is Fort Wayne?" as if they had tuned into a strange new part of the planet. Listo Fisher would take requests, explain patiently the physics and the atmospheric quirks that allowed the callers to hear themselves on the radio they were listening to, broadcast by a station days of travel away from where they were. "It's a miracle," some yahoo in a swamp would yodel.

One night in the middle of a beguine, a voice came on the radio speaking what I found out later was Spanish. For a moment in my sandbag state, I thought it must be part of the song, a conductor or an announcer turning to a ballroom full of people in a hotel, both the people and the hotel now long turned to dust and the evening just charged molecules on magnetic tape, saying to them good night and good-bye. Thank you for the lovely evening. We've been brought to you by United Fruit and now are returning you to your local studios. But the voice kept talking, rising and falling, the *r*'s rolling and the *k*'s clotting together. Every once and again I would recognize a word, its syllables all bitten through and the whole thing rounded out by a vowel that seemed endless, howling or whispered.

The telephone rang. It was three in the morning.

"What the hell is that?" my father asked. The words were in both my ears now. I could hear the speech in peaks playing on his radio across town, like a range of mountains floating above clouds.

"Dad, what are you doing up?"

"Listening to the radio when this blather came over it."

I asked him why he wasn't asleep instead. The radios continued to emit the speech, a rhythm had begun to emerge beneath the words, not unlike the beguine it had preempted. Just then there was a huge crash of static. I heard my father say, "What the," but it wasn't static, it was applause, and as it trailed off, I heard the voice say the same phrase over again a few times, starting up again, as the cheering subsided.

"Oh," my father said, "you're awake then."

"Of course, I'm awake," I lied to him. "You woke me up." I asked him again why he was awake.

"I haven't slept in years."

"Well, go to sleep, Dad."

"You go to sleep then."

"I am asleep. I've been asleep," I said.

"What's that crap on the radio?"

"Change the station, Dad. Maybe it's the station."

"But I always listen to WOWO."

I hung up and listened to WOWO. The speech continued for two more hours punctuated by bursts of applause, the sound then breaking into a chirping chant, steady at first, then going out of phase, melting back into itself, and the rising hiss of more applause. The voice would be there again. It seemed to plead or joke. It warned, begged. It egged on. It blamed and denied, sniffed its nose. It sneered. It promised. I could hear it tell a story. It explained what it had meant. It revised. It wooed. Toward the morning it grew hoarse. It grew hoarse and dried up. It wound up repeating a word, which seemed too long to me, again and again until that word was picked up by the listeners on the radio, who amplified it into a cloud of noise that this time was static. Then Bob Sievers was on the radio and his theme song was playing:

Let me lay my head on a bed of new mown hay, hey hey!

There are so many secrets in this world. About the time my husband, who I'll call David, and my best friend, who I'll call Linda, started sleeping together, two silver blimps were launched in a swamp south of a city I'll call Miami. They were tethered there to slabs of freshly cured concrete a thousand feet below. I think of those balloons floating there, drifting toward each other, perhaps bumping together finally, and rebounding in excruciating slow motion. The wires connecting them to the ground shored them up, I imagine, so their nuzzling was reigned in, the arc of rotation proscribed. They moved hugely, deliberately, like whales in a tropic bay. Their shadows shifted on the spongy ground below. I am almost asleep, dreaming, when the nodding blimps turn into the slick bodies of my husband and my best friend sliding beneath a skin of sheets, moving as deliberately and as coyly until they are tangled up in each other's embrace, and then that Zeppelin in New Jersey bursts into flames and melts into itself, the fire spilling from the night sky. There is a voice on the radio crying how horrible, how horrible to see the skeleton of the airship support, for an instant, a white skin of flames.

The curious in south Florida were told that the bobbing balloons were part of a weather experiment, a lie. Their real purpose was to hold aloft a radio antenna aimed at Cuba. It was propaganda radio. The voice I had heard was Castro's, Cuban radio's response, jamming the signal spilling south from the balloons, overflowing on the clear channel all the way north.

For a long time our government denied what was going on and the speeches continued through the night. I bought a Spanish-to-English dictionary and translated one word I'd catch out of the one thousand perhaps that flashed by, leafing through the book until I found something I thought sounded like what I had heard. He's talking about a ship, I'd think. And he is sitting or he sat once. Overlooking the sea specked with ships. Now there are roosters. Ships, the holds filled with roosters, who crow out the watch. Mothers waiting for the ships, I thought, at the docks, shielding their eyes in the sun, empty baskets balanced on their heads.

WOWO's ratings went up as people stayed awake late into the night to listen to the interruptions, the speeches with the static of applause. And, as if they realized they now had an audience, the programers in Havana began to salt the broadcast with cuts of Latin music, bosa novas and sambas, anthems and pretty folk songs plucked out on guitars with squeaky strings. Downtown, during the day, I began to see people napping at their desks, sleepwalking to the copying rooms and the coffee machines. More men smoked cigars. High school Spanish classes were assigned to listen to the station at night, meeting at their teachers' houses for slumber parties. So tired, we were infected by our dreams. The days grew warmer. I had been unable to sleep for so long the measured pace of the people around me matched my own endless daily swim through the thick, sunlit air. We moved like my cats, lounged and yawned, stared at each other with half-closed eyes.

I listened for Fidel at night. Over time, I counted on him. I translated his rambling monologues in my own dreamy way as he talked about his island with its green unpronounceable trees, the blooming pampas where butterflies from the north nested in the fall, lazy games of catch performed by children in starchy white uniforms chattering in a dialect that predates Columbus. You see, I was ready for someone to talk to me, to explain everything to me. How I looked like a movie star in those sunglasses I wore continually. How fires smell in the cane fields as the sugar carmelizes. I thought I understood romance for once, and martyrdom, maybe even revolution. This ropey language, the syrup of its sound, an elixir, was on the air now all the time, crept into my bed each night.

What would my father say? It filled me up, crowding out the mortgaged furniture, the old sad music, the phone calls to the police, and all the names, especially the names I've now forgotten were ever attached to those other frequencies through which I drifted.

◆▶

On Hoosier Hysteria

This is true. During the annual high school basketball tourna-
ments in Indiana, the winning small towns send a team to the
cities for the regional or state semifinals. Those towns empty
completely for the games, the whole population evacuated by
yellow buses and strings of private sedans and wagons. The Governor declares an emergency and sends a few state troopers or
a truckload of the Guard to patrol the deserted streets.

I got sent to Marion one spring when that team was playing
up in Fort Wayne. I was attached to a clerical unit stationed at
Fort Benjamin Harrison outside of Indianapolis. We convoyed
up from the south and parked on the outskirts of the ville as the
residents streamed north. We could hear the horns. A muscle
car sped by camouflaged with crepe paper and tempera. We were
humping it into town, two files, one to a gutter, along the main
street. The lieutenant sent a squad down a side street. Dogs
barked. Up ahead was the small downtown of two-storied stores
and offices. Hovering just above the brick buildings, a huge
water tower seemed to float like a dark cloud, its supporting legs
obscured by the buildings and trees. There was writing on its
side that couldn't be read from where I was, the town name and
zip code perhaps, the sense of it stretched around out of sight.

We had to hold the town for the day, and, if the team won its afternoon game, stay the night in bivouac set up on the high school football field.

It took us a few hours or so to walk the streets and rattle some door handles. Tacked up on every garage was a scuffed backboard and rotting net. I looked in the windows of the empty homes, saw the big glossy house and garden magazines scalloped on the coffee tables, the dish rag draped over the faucet in the kitchen, an old pitcher filled with pussy willow branches in the middle of the dining table. Some places were unlocked, and I poked my head in, shouting to make sure no one was there. As I walked through one house, I listened to the clocks ticking. There was Eckrich meat in the refrigerator. I turned on the television and stood in front of it as it warmed up. The game was on, live, the boys going through warm-up drills at each end of the court. Somewhere in the crowd, the people who lived in that house shook pom-poms behind the cheerleaders. I stood there, too close to the set, in the living room, in full gear, my helmet on my head, cradling my rifle in my arms. The boys in their shiny outfits did lay-up after lay-up. Each of them took a little skip as he started to break for the hoop, meeting the feeding pass in mid-stride, the ball then rolling off his fingers, kissing the glass. A sergeant tapped on the picture window. "Quayle," he said, his voice filtering into the house, "get your butt out here."

I followed a squad down an oiled street. The sidewalks had crumbled into dust. The Kiwanis had tapped the maple trees growing along the side of the road, the sap plunking inside the tin buckets. We formed up at the end of the block where the town met the surrounding field of corn stubble. The field went on for miles, broken only by a stand of trees, a cluster of buildings, a cloud of crows rising up from the ground. We stood there waiting for something to happen. How strange and empty the world had become. In a few more weeks spring would be here for good, but you would never guess it from the way things

the news of his character's nativity seeped into the cockpit of the car, we pounded fists on the padded dash, hooting and whistling. We flashed the car lights and honked the horn until the steering wheel rang. For several minutes, all the cars rocked and flashed, the blaring horns drowning out what was being said on screen. It seemed at any second these hunks of metal we rode in would rise up and come alive. But they didn't.

●▸

On the State
of the Union

The Speaker bangs the gavel for order. The gavel is a gift to the United States from the people of India, the largest democracy to the world's oldest. Order.

I'm standing in front of my swivel chair next to the Speaker. I'm the President of the Senate. At the beginning of his speech the President of the United States will call me Mr. President.

The party members are still on their feet. Some are whistling, fingers stretching lips, like fans at a basketball game. The red light bounces from camera to camera around the house. The Majority are settling in, looking before they sit, picking up the text that has been distributed to their seats. Some are riffling through its pages. Others are shouting into their neighbors' ears while they continue to applaud routinely. Order.

The gavel is made of pale marble and ivory fitted with brass trim. The Speaker rests his weight on his knuckles, the gavel's handle squeezed in one fist. He looks like my father, his chin lowered, looking out at the house through his bushy brow. It makes me want to do something bad, and the boys in our party on the floor start up again after the Speaker has introduced the President, just as much to see that stern mask set deeper on the Speaker's Neanderthal face as to cheer the President on.

I watch the red light on the cameras as it goes off and on around the room. I try to guess where it will alight next. The one in the lobby doorway. The one fixed on the mezzanine wall. The one behind the Speaker that shows the fanned seating of the floor. The angle that captures the various Secretaries and Generals and Ambassadors. I never know when the camera will focus on me. I am looking thoughtful, I think, as I applaud. The light flickers on the camera aimed at the wives in the gallery above. I follow the vector from that camera, its lense slowly extending for a tight close-up on the First Lady, who stands by the railing in the blue dress with big buttons, pearls bubbling at her throat, her eyes glassy, as always, applauding effortlessly. I see her over the President's right shoulder as she smooths her skirt around her hips as she sits down. And we all sit down.

Her husband begins to speak, and I remind myself to count the number of times he will be interrupted by applause. I know the words that are cues. The Whips have briefed us in caucus. There are plants salted in the gallery to trigger responses. The pauses are scripted. I always tell myself that I will keep track of the applause to match the number with the talking heads at the networks. But I lose track. My thoughts flit away from me like that light that now burns on the camera in the center aisle below us, suddenly extinguishing itself and suddenly flaring up again after completing a circuit of the room during an interlude of cheering.

They've been working on the President. I can see the line of pancake on his neck where the napkin masked his white collar. Color has been brushed on the cheek he turns toward me when his head scans the room. His hair is freshly dyed, the television lights polishing the contours, each strand lacquered into place.

I know what people are thinking. They see me brooding behind the President. I have touched up my own temples with a hint of gray. It is important that we all forget about the President's mortality. I alone am allowed to age. I imagine the Members on the floor squirming in their seats, adjusting their angles of vision, using the bulk of the President to blot me and then the thought of me out of their minds. The President's most recent collapse, captured on television, has brought me back into their thoughts that now are drifting away from the prepared text, the paragraph on infrastructure they have been following halfheartedly, and into that percentage of every minute each has allotted to daydream, fantasy, or prayer. I walk in the corridors of some skulls out there. The possibility of me. The blue-eyed, bushy-tailed fact of me.

To get back at them, I employ the old Toastmaster trick of imagining the audience naked, and they sit there like dollops of frosting, their famous gray heads collapsing into puddles of fat that fill the seat. The esteemed colleague from Rhode Island is a smear of freckles. There, Howie has a rash that itches. I see secret tattoos. Trickles of sweat deliberately trace the topography of Teddy's sagging breast. The thighs worn smooth, shiny, and white by a life dedicated to always wearing trousers straddles the shriveled assortment of penises, the Members' members, that now are listening to their owners' own state of the union, a message of hope and resurrection punctuated by a worn catalogue of past and very private images. Order. Order.

Up on the toes of their naked feet, cheering, their flesh jiggles and sways, breaks out in splotches of color. Bill's thighs have been stripped of veins for his bypass. The gentleman from New Jersey has new plugs. They are otherwise unremarkable, marked only for death they have convinced themselves for now does not exist for them. The cancer ticks in a chest, a strangled heart, a brain that forgets to remember. There is another nakedness beneath the twill layer of beige skin. And it is, perhaps, only accessible to me from my strange vantage on this dais looking out at them all. I see into them. My job description gives me this vision since all I do is wait on death. I am the official mourner. The shadow of death cast a few polite paces behind the aging President.

Above us all, the First Lady, also naked, her face framed by an aurora of hair, rises from her seat and continues to rise to hover near the ceiling. A gesture of etched lines divides her body into hemispheres of breasts and belly and clefts of her butt, a kind of ancient statue, veined marble and ivory. She cleaves apart suddenly. The parts whirling into a system of orbiting planets. The President looks up at the glowing constellation of his wife.

The President's speech continues. All of it has already been distributed. It is being delivered as if by a machine. I witness the essential part of him leave himself for a moment, shedding the shell of his suit, to float up above the august chamber of the House of Representatives, joining the animated and precious flesh of his wife.

I think such thoughts because the President thinks such thoughts. Much of what we do is fantasy. It is my job to dream his dreams. In case he is unable to complete his constitutional duties, I am ready to step into his place.

I chair, at the pleasure of the President, a commission on Space. I see in his dark suit the deep black fabric of the universe. There are still flakes of white dandruff on the shoulders and the back. I stare into the depths between those flecks of white transforming into twinkling stars. It is a map of heavenly bodies. This vacuum has a texture. I lose my way in its blackness. I no longer hear the speech. On television, I will appear lost in grave thought. I have forgotten the spontaneous applause. The infinite silence between those stars terrifies me.

MICHAEL MARTONE is the author and editor of several works of fiction and nonfiction. He and his wife, the poet Theresa Pappas, are publishers of Story County Books.